Midnight Gardens

By

Ellen Dugan

Published by Ellen Dugan

ACKKNOWLEDGMENTS

As always, thanks to my family, friends, beta readers, and editors.

Gypsy Spirit, Book 2

DAUGHTERS OF MIDNIGHT SERIES

Midnight Gardens, Book 1

Midnight Masquerade, Book 2 (Coming Soon)

Midnight Prophecy, Book 3 (Coming Soon)

If you look the right way, you can see that the whole world is a garden.

-Frances Hodgson Burnett, *The Secret Garden*

PROLOGUE

It seemed only right that I take a moment for myself. The drive home from Chicago had been long, and as I traveled down the Great River Road I was surprised at the wave of emotion that gripped me.

The soaring limestone bluffs pitted with curves and overhangs pushed the scenic road to the very edge of the river. As I drove, the Mississippi river to my left was bluer than I remembered, and the trees that scrambled up the opposite side of the road in defiance of those carved bluffs were hazed with early spring leaves.

With a sigh of relief, I pulled my car into the ferry parking lot. All day, every day, the ferries were open to those who wanted to beat the traffic on the Alton bridge, or for tourists who simply wanted to enjoy a picturesque ride across the rivers. When I left Ames Crossing three years before, I'd stopped here for one last look at the spot where the Illinois and Mississippi rivers met.

I climbed from my car and the wind was a shocking slap to the senses. Even in April the air was sharp and cold. I pocketed my keys, ignored the light rain that had begun to fall, and pushed my hands down in my jacket pockets. Facing the wind, I let myself take in the scene and tried to settle my thoughts.

As I stood, a bald eagle swooped down over the river, his talons splashing in the water. Smoothly he was airborne again, with a fish as his prize. I heard the click of camera phones and the delighted gasps of a few tourists who'd been waiting beside their cars for the next ferry ride to Missouri.

The ferry docked and the tourists started up their cars and began easing down toward the ramp. As I stood looking out over the water, the sun disappeared behind the gathering clouds. The light changed beautifully, becoming soft, misty and gray. Gulls were calling and gathering, hoping for a handout; and I continued to stand in the rain, letting the elements of air and water soothe me like nothing else could have.

Secretly glad I had the place to myself for a moment, I walked closer to the water. The wind had tears streaming from my eyes, but the chilly rain cleared my head and gave me some perspective. I tossed my hair away from my face. "Turn the page, Drusilla," I murmured. "Start a fresh chapter and see what new story unfolds." Amused at myself for thinking in writing metaphors, I turned to leave and suddenly halted, with the discovery that I wasn't alone after all.

A man stood off to the side. Like me he was facing the water, and the wind coming off the water had tossed his brown hair into a tumble of curls. The collar of his dark wool coat was popped against the cold. It accentuated a face that was narrow, yet oddly handsome. For a second, he reminded me a bit of a modern-day Heathcliff, standing there all broody and mysterious in defiance of the weather.

He turned his head, our eyes met, and my stomach gave one hard lurch. In recognition, or maybe even destiny, I wasn't sure. But whatever it was made me suck in a hard breath, and any polite greeting I might have made dried up on my tongue.

His eyes. Was my one clear thought.

I'd never seen eyes so intensely blue. I blinked, thinking it a trick of the misty light. But the man stared, studying me as closely as I studied him. A little spooked, I forced myself to nod politely. "Hello." I said, walking past him.

Silently, he continued to keep me in his line of sight as I walked back to my car.

Hands sweating, I fumbled for the key fob in my pocket. I pressed the button, the locks popped, and I quickly slid inside my vehicle. As I started up my car, I noted the man had again shifted his attention back to the water. His legs were planted, and his long dark coat was flapping in the wind coming off the river.

I swiped raindrops from my bangs, got settled and automatically flipped on the car stereo. Heart's "Magic Man" was playing. The song gave me a bit of a jolt, and I squinted down at the radio in surprise. Glancing back up, I discovered that the mysterious man had vanished.

I shifted in my seat, checking to see where he'd gone, but I didn't see him anywhere. My imagination bounced, and for a wild second I wondered if he was a mystical Selkie, or perhaps a male Siren that had emerged from the waters only to disappear as strangely as he'd arrived...

"Save it for your books, Dru." I shook my head over my imagination that a water spirit would have manifested on the shores of Illinois and eased the car out of the lot.

Singing along with Ann Wilson, I turned my car toward home and wondered what other surprises awaited me.

CHAPTER ONE

It had been a few years since I'd last been to my family home in Ames Crossing, Illinois. Tucked against the bluffs of the Mississippi river, our village was on the National Register of Historic Places. The hamlet was well known for its charming, curvy streets that wound their way up a steep hill, and a dozen quirky, vintage homes.

The village was a hodgepodge of different architectural styles that made no sense when seen all together. We had classic Victorians, a brick Italianate manor, farmhouse style homes, a few old stone houses with mansard roofs, and stone saltboxes that boasted colonial flair. This rather eccentric architectural jumble somehow added to the pretty storybook quality of our township, and it drew in tourists like a magnet.

Our property was situated just outside of the township proper, but currently the exterior of my family's farmhouse looked less like a story book and more like something straight out of a horror movie.

I frowned up at the façade of what used to be a pretty two-story farmhouse. "What in the world happened to Gran's house?"

Now, a gardener knows that nature will have its way. You can nurture, coax and tend your flowers and herbs in the garden; but in the end, the elements and the seasons will ultimately decide the plant's fate. For example, an early frost might decimate the delicate impatiens that provide a splash of color in a shady bed. Likewise, a spring that is too wet might cause black spot that ruins your heirloom roses...

And at the moment, the word *ruin* seemed completely appropriate.

I shut my eyes, waited for a five count and reopened them. "Damn it," I said. "It's still bad." The once crisp white siding looked dingy, and the paint on the trim was peeling. Shutters that used to be a vibrant blue hung crooked on the second floor, and I noticed that one large shutter was missing from the living room windows altogether.

Even more appalling was the state of the gardens. Although it was April, I expected to see daffodils fluttering in the flower beds and tulips breaking the ground in front of the neat emerald green boxwood hedges, like always.

But to my shock, I did not. The cottage garden my paternal grandmother had once lovingly tended—was all but gone. Swallowed up by overgrown plants and suffocated by what had to have been a year's worth of weeds.

"Well, isn't this a fine welcome home." My mysterious encounter with that spooky-eyed man at the river's edge slid away. I slammed the car door shut and stalked around to the passenger side to retrieve my purse, laptop case and two suitcases.

Old, dormant, and dried out tendrils from an autumn clematis gone wild snagged my jacket as I rolled the suitcases up the driveway. Stopping, I pulled my long blonde hair away from the problematic vines and over my far shoulder. As I paused, a robin began to sing from somewhere hidden within the hedge.

I leaned in closer. There were a few branches bravely peeking out from underneath the smothering clematis. I ran my fingertips over a soft bud. The classic hedge symbolized rest and recovery, I remembered. But now, only a gray haze of what had once been gorgeous pussy willow hedges were still visible.

The gardens weren't ruined, only ignored. I told myself. Reaching out, I ran my fingers over more of the fuzzy buds. "Neglected and passed over, eh?" I said to the shrubs. "I know exactly how you feel."

I shook my head, amazed at the disrepair of the house and grounds, wondering what other surprises awaited me inside. Taking a deep breath, I ordered myself to remain positive. "It will be alright. You're home. All you need is a fresh start." *And...*I admitted, hitching the strap of my laptop case higher over my shoulder, *time. Time to heal and time to pull myself back together.*

The front door slammed open. "Dru!" My little sister Camilla launched herself out of the door, down the steps, and straight into my arms.

"You're here!"

"Hi Cammy!" I hugged her every bit as hard as she did me. After a few moments, I pulled her back and held her at arms length. "Wow, I love your hair! It's great!"

"Thanks." Cammy said, tucking a section of platinum blonde hair behind her ear. Her hair was cut in a sassy bob and was made only more striking by the unexpected color that ran through it.

"I saw the pictures on your social media page but...holy cats, girl." I took her chin in my hand. "Bubblegum pink. Nobody else could pull that off but you."

"I took a chance with the color." Cammy tilted her head. "I really love it."

"And you pierced your nose." I grinned at the thin silver hoop. "You're brave, I'll give you that."

"You're brave too," Cammy said, giving me another hug. "You finally shook off that asshole and came back to Ames Crossing."

"Yes indeed." Even as my stomach lurched, I forced a cheerful tone of voice. "I've left Chicago, am officially divorced, and *very* glad to be home."

"I wish you'd have let me come out there Dru. I'd have helped you get your things together."

"I only took my computers, clothes and personal items," I tried to explain. "I didn't want anything else."

"Please tell me that you trashed that cheating bastard's lake view apartment when you moved out."

I laughed, slightly. "Hate to disappoint you, Cam."

"Did you at least cut holes in his designer clothes, and pour all his snotty French champagne down the kitchen sink? Tell me you took golf clubs to the hood of his sports car."

"That sounds like a Taylor Swift music video." I patted her cheek. "No. I didn't."

"You're breaking my heart, Dru."

"I got a hell of a divorce settlement." I flashed a brittle smile. "I promise you, that hurt him far, far worse."

"Good." Cammy nodded. "Because you have no idea how tempted I've been to go after him with magick."

I blinked at her. "Wait, isn't that against your Wiccan beliefs?"

"Yeah, well." Cammy buffed her nails on her raspberry colored sweater. "Technically, I'm not a Wiccan."

"Oh?' I tried to keep up. "I thought you were. I even read up on that."

"Aww, that was sweet of you." Cammy grabbed a suitcase and hauled it up the porch steps.

"Well, when my baby sister goes off to grad school and joins a coven, it was the least I could do." I huffed out, hauling the remaining case up to stand beside her.

"Technically, I consider myself a Witch," she said.

"So, what, you're like one of the dark sisters now?" I wiggled my eyebrows. "Gran's going to be very proud."

"Hey." Cammy nudged me with an elbow. "She actually *is* proud. Remember, we come from a long line of herbalists, healers—"

"And wise women." I finished the line for her. "Good grief. You sounded exactly like Gran when you said that."

Cammy flashed a smile and pushed open the front door. "Call me a Pagan, wise woman, or a Witch. Either way, you better believe that if you mess with one of my sisters—I'll go medieval on your ass."

I couldn't help the snort of laughter that escaped. "God, I've missed you." I grabbed the handle of my bag and rolled it through the front door. "How is Gran?"

Cammy rolled my other suitcase inside. "She's weaker than she likes to admit. It was a tough eight months and a long recovery. First the broken hip, and hip replacement surgery, then her coming down with pneumonia this winter."

Guilt all but smothered me. "I'm sorry I couldn't be here these last few months. I tried to—"

Cammy's green eyes narrowed as she cut me off. "Shut up, Drusilla. You were dealing with the divorce—we all knew. The only one who put pressure on you—was you. Besides, the money you sent every month really helped out. Because of that, we were able to have a nurse come visit twice a week while Gran was recovering."

"Seeing the state of the grounds makes me wish I could have done more."

Cammy reached out and pulled a piece of dried clematis vine from my hair. "Has the garden been complaining to you already?"

I took the tendril of dried vine back from Camilla. "Apparently."

My sister ran a hand down my arm. "I know the property looks rough, but we got through it. Besides, Gran is doing much better now. We had her sitting out on the front porch a few days ago. She said the sunshine did her more good than the physical therapy Gabriella drives her to."

As my youngest sister closed the door I glanced around, and my shoulders dropped in relief. The interior of the house was as welcoming and pretty as the outside was not, and it smelled sweetly of the lavender pot pourri my Gran always made.

My gaze took in the gleaming hardwood floors and the spotless front rooms. The brown overstuffed leather sofa beckoned with plump linen accent pillows. The walls had been repainted since my last visit home and were now a warm ivory. To ward off the early spring chill, a fire burned low in the brick fireplace.

"It looks great in here." I set my purse aside on the rustic farm table the family used as a console in the foyer. The banister leading to the second floor shone in the afternoon light, and there wasn't a speck of dust in sight.

"You sound surprised." Cammy raised a single darkened eyebrow. It was a move she was particularly proud of.

"After seeing the outside of the house..." I trailed off.

Camilla winced. "I'm sorry. I came home on weekends and helped out as often as I could while Gran was recuperating."

"What about Mom, did she come by and help out at all?"

Cammy grimaced. "Nope. Mom took off for a cruise around the world with her new boyfriend before the holidays. Haven't heard much from her since."

"I expect she's hoping for husband number four." I eased the strap off my shoulder and set the laptop case aside. "Ironic isn't it, how I always swore I'd never end up like Mom, yet here I am, divorced and moving back home?"

"You're nothing like our mother." Cammy's voice was fierce. "You'd never abandon your own children."

Her words caused me to wince. *Not that I could have children...but still.*

"I was little, but I remember," Cammy said. "After Daddy died, Mom pretty much dumped us on Gran."

"And thank god for it." I studied the foyer of the old house I'd grown up in. "She gave us a good life, while Mom was off doing whatever it is she does."

"We were lucky," my sister said. "Now it's our turn to take care of Gran."

"What happened to the gardens?" I asked quietly. "Gran would sure as hell never allow her herbs and flowers to be neglected like that."

"Well you know Gabriella." Cammy let her hands fall. "She's a whiz *in* the house, cooking, designing, and decorating—but she hates getting her hands in the dirt outside."

"I was busy working and taking care of Gran." A soft voice came from the direction of the staircase. "There wasn't a lot of time left for yard work."

Unfazed at being overheard, Camilla grinned. "Hey Gabriella! Dru's home!"

I watched my middle sister come down the steps from the second floor. Her hair was a pale blonde and flowed in waves around her face. Solemn, blue eyes regarded me steadily, but there was no smile. "I thought Gran's well being was more important than weeding the flower beds," she said, "and I did manage to keep the formal herb garden out back tended."

There was a slight bite to her tone as she stopped on the last riser. Most people wouldn't have caught it—but this was my sister. I knew her expressions and tone of voice almost as well as my own.

Duly chastised, I nodded. "I'm thankful you were here, especially since I couldn't be."

Gabriella didn't jump to hug me as Camilla had. Instead she stayed on the bottom step, just out of reach. "Your things were delivered yesterday," she said, calmly. "I had them stack the moving boxes in your old room."

"Thank you." I tried a smile. "How are you,

Ella?" I used her childhood nickname.

"Fine," her lips curved up a bit. "Gran's been pretty excited to have you move back home." As she spoke a gray tabby came down the steps. It peered up at me, and its eyes were as deep a blue as Gabriella's.

"Hi Shadow," I greeted the cat. The fluffy cat was not impressed. He tucked himself between my sister's feet and the stair tread, peeking out from around her legs.

"Drusilla."

At the sound of my name I turned to find Gran. She was cruising slowly down the hallway from the back of the house with the aid of a walker. She walked proudly forward and was rocking dark gray workout pants and a zippered hot pink jacket.

"Hello, Gorgeous!" I cried, going straight to my grandmother. I gave her a careful hug.

"There's my girl." My grandmother ran a hand down my long hair. "Finally, you're home," Gran said with a catch in her throat.

"I'm sorry. It took longer than expected to...settle everything," I apologized.

I eased back and studied the woman who had

raised me. Gran's ash blonde hair brushed her shoulders. It was casually styled, and though her face was thinner, her eyes were still the same. Warm, wise and midnight blue, even if the crinkles at the corners were more pronounced.

"Well, you're home now, where you belong." She gave my shoulder a squeeze. "The daughters of Midnight are all together again and under one roof," she said. "This calls for a celebration."

"No whiskey, Grandma," Cammy said sternly.

"I'm not an invalid dear." Priscilla Midnight raised her perfectly arched brows. "You wait and see...in two weeks I'll rid myself of this silly walker."

Gabriella put her hands on her hips. "That depends on what the therapist says."

"Bah!" Gran tossed her head. "I'm as healthy as a horse."

Cammy rolled her dark rimmed eyes. "Here we go."

I stepped into the fray, "I've been dying for a cup of your special peppermint and chamomile tea, Gran. Let's go sit in the kitchen and have some."

In short order, my Gran was seated in her cushioned chair at the head of the table, and Camilla plopped herself down next to me. She grabbed my hand, admired my manicure, and proceeded to tell me all about her life at college. Between her classes and studies, Cammy had established a campus paranormal investigation team...

Which knowing my sister's fascination with the occult, really didn't surprise me.

Meanwhile, Gabriella bustled around the kitchen territorially, serving sugar cookies and making a pot of tea. Shadow the cat lived up to his name and followed my sister around silently.

I sat back in my chair, letting the scents of the herbs drying overhead soothe my nerves. The voices of my family washed over me, and I was grateful to be back.

CHAPTER TWO

My old room hadn't changed much. It faced the front of the house, and its slanting walls were low and charming. It was comforting somehow, to find the faded floral wallpaper with its sprigs of lily-of-the-valley, and the same old wrought iron double bed I'd grown up with, waiting for me. A pretty patchwork quilt in faded blues and greens was spread across the bed, and my dresser was painted a sage green now. The old wooden desk I once used as a student was still tucked under the eaves on the opposite side of the room, and a half dozen cardboard moving boxes took up most of the floor space.

Cammy had helped me haul my suitcases upstairs after tea, took one gander at the mountain of boxes, and announced she had a meeting with her fellow ghost hunters and needed to be back on campus.

I smiled. "Of course you do."

"Hey, don't knock it," Cammy said. "I've seen some pretty interesting things in the past few years."

"I guess your fascination with ghosts is all my fault." I slung my arm around her neck and gave her a hug. "I'm the one who talked you into going up to the old Marquette place on Notch Cliff when we were teenagers."

"Saw my first ghost that night and have been studying hauntings ever since." Camilla winked.

"Thanks for being here today," I said.

"Of course. Welcome home, Dru." She kissed my cheek and got the hell out of Dodge.

I really didn't blame her. With a tired sigh I carefully placed my laptop case on the desk, then went and sat on the edge of the bed. I glanced over at my reflection in the oval mirror above the dresser and started a critical assessment of my appearance. The woman who stared back at me was still Chicago Drusilla;

and while physically she appeared to be fine, emotionally she was a wreck.

Chicago Drusilla had worn pretty, expensive clothes, had done the occasional book signing at posh shops, and read to children's groups at the main branch of the public library. She'd learned to play tennis and could make small talk with the best of them. She'd had regular mani-pedis, glossy, perfectly styled hair, lived in an amazing lakefront apartment, and had the luxury of working from home...a life most women would kill for.

And that world had come crashing down slowly but surely when she couldn't give her husband the one little thing they both wanted, no matter how hard she'd tried.

"You're thinking about yourself in the third person, Drusilla." I said to my reflection. "And now I'm talking to myself, *again*." With a groan, I dropped my face in my hands and started to laugh.

It was either that, or break down and sob.

Thanks to my divorce settlement, I could afford to take a few months off before starting my next manuscript. After seeing the state of the property...I'd immediately made up my mind to use this opportunity and devote my time to restoring the family gardens. They were my grandmother's pride and joy, and the inspiration behind my career.

Yes, it would be hard work, I accepted that. However, it would be good for me, and I relished the opportunity to get my hands in the soil again.

I considered my pampered hands. They'd toughen up fast enough, and I could always wear gloves to protect my nails. Right now they were long, filed in a squared-off oval, and painted in a sparkling green. "Spring green," I decided.

My fingernails were my one silly indulgence that I was going to try and keep. Everything else from my Chicago life was going to go. I was swapping back to my trusty jeans, sweatshirts, boots and tennis shoes. Feeling better with some sort of plan, I grabbed the nearest box, ripped off the packing tape and began to unpack.

Several hours later, night had fallen. Comfortable in my old jeans, sweatshirt and trainers, I hauled the broken-down boxes across the back gardens and past the circular formal herb garden that Gabriella had manage to maintain. Pausing, I ran my fingers over the gray dormant foliage of a huge lavender plant. The clean fragrance brought back memories of Gran creating her herbal soaps, salves and lotions. She'd sold them for years, every Saturday at the local farmer's market, all from the herbs and flowers grown in her own yard.

Smiling to myself, I moved on toward the detached garage and my potting shed. The sidewalks were clear, and the bit of lawn on either side of the pathway had obviously been mowed at some point. The solar lights added ambiance, but half of them were crooked in the ground, and a few weren't working at all.

I took a critical study of the massive job I faced. The perennial gardens and beds for the flowers that Gran prized were completely overgrown and as choked with weeds as the front beds were. The big gazebo my grandfather had built before he'd passed away ten years ago was still solid. It stood off to the far left, but obviously hadn't had any attention in a while.

The roses planted around the gazebo, I noted, were in desperate need of pruning.

Sadly, the faery theme garden that had inspired my first book was completely engulfed by tall grass and dead weeds. I made my way across the grass and stood, surveying what was left of what *had* been my favorite part of the gardens. Narrowing my eyes, I estimated where the old faery statue should be and reached in.

Sure enough, the concrete statue of the little sprite reading a book was still there. I took a few moments, set the boxes aside, and pulled out the weeds from around her until I had a small section clear. "Hello, Bluebell," I said. *Bluebell* was the name I'd given the statue as a young girl. Now, she was the inspiration for the faery heroine of my children's books.

A clutch of wild violets had sprouted up in the garden, and I plucked a few flowers and laid them across the open book in the statue's hands as a sort of offering to the nature spirits in the garden. "I'm sorry I wasn't here to tend your bower," I said quietly, straightening a solar light by pushing the stake more firmly back into the soil.

"But I'm home now, and everything will change." No sooner had the words left my mouth than a breeze whipped through the gardens. Wind chimes rang out on the breeze, and I nodded my head in acknowledgment that the elementals had heard and accepted my vow.

Picking up the cardboard, I considered where to start the restoration as I went to stack the boxes against the recycle bins. My task complete, I made my way back toward the potting shed. The shed had been my domain when I'd lived here. Now after witnessing the state of the yard, I questioned what sort of shape the rustic building would be in.

An old weathered sign hung above the door stating the building to be *Dru's Shed*. Cammy had made the sign for me a decade ago, and while it was faded, it was still there.

Sorcerer's violet scrambled up the side of the old wooden shed. The shade loving plant also known as *Vinca minor* had almost entirely covered the north wall of the building. A few shoots had even worked their way inside a window.

"Pleasures of memory," I said, delighted that

I'd remembered the old meaning of the herb. I'd had many happy hours working in that shed. First at the elbow of my grandparents, and then later, on my own. With a smile, I opened the blue painted door. I felt around for the lights and flipped on the switch, wondering what I would find.

The sturdy wooden work bench was dusty and messy. Terra cotta pots and hand tools were piled across the work bench. Large bags of compost and mulch were stacked messily on the brick floor. The wheel barrow was leaning upright against the far wall, and I noted the shovel, hoe, and other tools were stacked, handles down, in an old metal garbage can. I stepped farther inside and spotted a large stack of yard waste bags. "Excellent," I said. "That's going to save me a trip to the hardware store."

Beside the bags, a food and water bowl rested, and I wondered why Shadow had bowls in the potting shed. When I caught movement out of the corner of my eye, I jumped back with a startled squeal. A pretty tortoiseshell cat peeked her head around from behind the bags of mulch. She was followed by three, four, no...five kittens. The family all came prancing out, meowing noisily.

"Well, hello." I knelt down to meet the tenants. Apparently the mother had taken advantage of an old, empty cardboard box for her family. "Aren't you all cute? Ella took you in, eh?"

The kittens were a mixture of patterns. Three were white with random orange or black patches, one was a tabby, and another had the same tortoiseshell markings as her mother.

I'd always loved babies, of any kind. I couldn't help but coo over the kittens. Mama cat was friendly enough, so I sat on the dusty brick floor and indulged myself in a bit of kitten therapy. I'd had maybe five minutes with the kittens when the wooden door swung open. I had expected to see my sister, and instead was confronted by a stranger.

A young girl stood in the doorway. "What are you doing in here?" she demanded.

"I live here. What are *you* doing here?" I asked the girl. I'd never seen the child before. She had reddish blonde hair held back from her face by a navy headband. A smattering of freckles decorated her pale skin. *What was she...ten or eleven years old?*

"You don't live here." Her haughty tone of voice went perfectly with an upper crust east coast accent. "Mrs. Midnight and Gabriella live here."

"I'm Gabriella's sister."

She snorted in derision and rolled her eyes. "No you're not. I've met Cammy."

I stayed where I was, with kittens crawling all over my lap. "Well, allow me to introduce myself," I said. "I'm Dru. Drusilla Midnight."

"Oh." She looked down her nose. "You're the one that got divorced."

I raised my brows. "That would be me."

"Gabriella said, you lived in Chicago."

"That's correct." I nodded. "Since you know about me, why don't you tell me who you are?"

Hydrangea blue eyes met mine in a sort of stare down, but she didn't answer.

"Okay, let's try this," I said. "Where are you from?"

She folded her arms over a fancy navy blue blazer. "I live on the neighboring estate."

Neighboring estate? I frowned over the

phrase. *Only a trust fund kid could say that and not sound ridiculous.* The only other house nearby was the old Italianate brick home. The last time I'd seen it, the place had been empty and in need of repair. "Did your parents purchase the old Crawford place?"

"No. My parents didn't buy anything, and I came to see the kittens. Gabriella said I could, whenever I wanted." She plopped down on the bricks, uncaring of her clothes. She picked up a kitten and sent a scowl my way. "You can leave now."

"Do your parents know you're here?" I asked, leaning back against the big bags of compost as if I had all the time in the world.

"My parents are dead." There was no inflection to the words. None at all. "My guardian bought the old Crawford house," she continued, "and I got stuck here."

Those hard words had me eyeballing the girl. "I see." The kittens obviously were familiar with the girl. *En masse* they abandoned me to climb all over her.

I stood up and brushed off my jeans. "So, you're our neighbor."

"Obviously."

"Well aren't you charming?" I shook my head at her attitude and reached for the door handle. "Do you want me to leave the door—"

"Shut the door on your way out," she cut me off.

Any sympathy I might have had for the girl was snuffed out by her snotty attitude. "Goodnight then," I said, and shut the door quietly behind me.

I started down the path back toward the house, intent on hunting up my sister and finding out more about the girl. But I didn't have to search at all, Gabriella was on the back porch waiting for me.

"Was that Brooke?" she asked.

"That depends," I said. "Is she a tween with ginger hair, a Boston accent, and bad attitude?" I asked.

Her lips twitched. "That would be Brooke James."

"I just met the little princess."

"I'll bet her guardian doesn't know she's here. She probably slipped out again." Gabriella sighed.

Automatically, I swung my eyes toward the nearest house. A good acre stood between our farmhouse and the old Italianate brick home. "Did the girl walk all the way here by herself—in the dark?"

"Probably," my sister said. "I'll go call him."

Despite myself, I was curious, and I followed Gabriella into the kitchen and eavesdropped shamelessly on the conversation.

My grandmother still had an old landline phone, and Gabriella stood twirling the phone cord in her finger as she spoke. "You're welcome, Garrett. Yes. I'll have Brooke out front when you arrive."

"Garrett?" I asked.

"Garrett Rivers." Gabriella hung up the phone. "He and his business partner are the ones who bought the Crawford house last year. It's completely renovated now. Garrett's nice, and Gran's crazy about him."

The old house had supposedly been a show stopper once upon a time with its fancy Italianate architecture, cupola, and scenic view of the Mississippi river. It seemed like the perfect place for an older gentleman to renovate. "The girl said she lives with her guardian?" I asked as Gran came cruising into the kitchen with her walker.

My sister nodded. "Yes, she does."

Hmmm, I thought. *Maybe he was an established old bachelor, and out of his depth dealing with a young girl?* "What's this Mr. Rivers like?" I started to ask.

"Did Brooke slip out again?" Gran wanted to know.

"She's in the shed with the kittens," I said. "Do you want me to go get her?"

"No." Gran put her hand on my arm. "You let me take care of this. I know a few things about dealing with difficult girls."

"I was never difficult." I planted my hands on my hips and dove into the old family argument. "I was the best behaved out of the three of us."

Gran threw back her head and laughed. "Sweetheart, it's adorable that you think so."

"Ella's always been the troublemaker." I teased my quiet sister.

She took the bait. "I was *not*. It was Camilla who was always in trouble. With you egging her on."

Gran shook her head at the two of us razzing each other and made her way to the back door. She opened it and called for Brooke to come inside. A minute later Brooke came into our kitchen, and to my surprise held the door for my Gran, allowing her to more easily maneuver her walker.

"Brooke, your uncle is on his way to pick you up," Gran said while the girl pouted. "Now you know you are welcome to drop by any time —"

"He's not really my uncle," Brooke interjected. "He's my legal guardian."

Gran went on smoothly as if she hadn't been interrupted. "Be that as it may, I *must* insist that in the future you let Garrett know where you are."

Brooke set her jaw. "He's never home anyway. He doesn't care about me."

"Your word, Brooke." Gran insisted. "You'll let him know that you're here from now on."

"Fine." Brooke scowled.

Gran nodded at the terse word and started to shift her weight. Suddenly she stumbled, and before I could make a grab for her, Brooke had taken her by the elbow.

"Oh thank you, Brooke." My grandmother's voice was uncharacteristically high and breathy. "Do you suppose you could help me to the living room, so I could put my feet up?"

"Yes, ma'am." Brooke carefully guided my Gran down the hall, and toward the front of the house.

I shot a concerned glance at my sister. "Is Gran that weak?"

Gabriella bit her lip. "Not at all. She's playing up the 'old lady with a walker' bit to distract Brooke."

"Really?"

"You know our Gran." My sister's lips curved. "She's a canny old bird."

"I have to see the rest of this act for myself." I went straight down the hall, past Gran's first floor bedroom and into the living room, where Brooke was arranging the couch pillows for my grandmother.

"Thank you, Brooke." Gran's voice was still breathy, and behind the kid's back I sent my grandmother a look. While Brooke was occupied fetching the remote for the television, Gran raised a single eyebrow. I bit my lip against a laugh while Brooke fussed over her. Headlights from a car flashed in the front windows a few minutes later, and Gran sat up straight, patting her hair into place.

Was she primping? I smothered a grin. When a knock sounded on the front door, Brooke turned her face away and deliberately stared at the wall.

I went to the front door fully expecting to see an older, distinguished gentleman, however the man who stood on our front porch had my jaw dropping open in surprise.

It was the man I'd seen down at the ferry dock. I swiftly estimated him to be in his late thirties—and as I'd gathered the very first time I'd seen him, he was tall, trim and well...he was gorgeous.

Our eyes locked, and I blinked. "It's you."

Well," he said, smiling slightly. "Hello again."

I knew expensive and custom-tailored clothes when I saw them, and they only accentuated the rest of the package. His brown hair showed a bit of a wave. Sharp cheekbones were very prominent in his narrow face, and the eyes that met mine were indeed a mercurial shade of blue-green. "Can I help you?" I asked automatically.

"I'm Garrett Rivers."

I did my best not to stammer. "*You're* Mr. Rivers?"

"I am," he said, and his brows drew together in impatience. "I'm here to fetch Brooke."

CHAPTER THREE

My sister stepped smoothly forward. "Hi Garrett, come on in."

"Gabriella." Garrett Rivers nodded. "How are you?"

"I'm fine." She motioned for him to come inside. "This is my sister, Drusilla." Gabriella made the introductions smoothly.

"Hello," I said, and struggled to compose myself. He crossed the threshold, and I felt my heart give one hard jerk in reaction. *Definitely a flesh and blood man,* I realized. *Not a water spirit.* I stood back, subtly checking out our elegant guest. I shouldn't have tried to be discreet, because he promptly ignored me.

"I'm sorry about this." Garrett stepped into the foyer and moved towards the living room.

He nodded to Gran. "Mrs. Midnight, good evening."

Gran waved. "Hello Garrett."

He smiled at Gran, but his eyes narrowed as he spotted Brooke sitting in a chair with her face averted. "Brooke," he began, "you have got to stop taking off whenever you feel like it."

In response, Brooke sniffed and jerked her face farther away from him.

"Brooke," Garrett said. "We've interrupted the Midnight's evening enough. Let's go back to the house."

Brooke ignored him.

"Young lady, I arrive home after a very long day, and Mrs. Huntley tells me that you're missing. Again." Garrett dragged a hand through his hair. "I've really had about enough of your games."

Brooke shifted, crossing her arms over her chest and sticking out her chin. "You can't make me go anywhere."

"Brooke!" Garrett Rivers snapped his fingers and pointed towards the front door. "Let's go!"

"Now just a minute!" I couldn't help it, and jumped right in. "That is no way to speak to a child."

Garrett Rivers looked daggers at me. "You're *not* helping the situation," he said through his teeth.

"And neither are you." I pointed out.

"Oh, I'm sorry." His tone was acid. "I didn't realize I was in the presence of a parenting expert."

"No, I'm not an expert." The barb hit home harder than he could have ever known, and purposefully, I lowered my voice. "But even I know that snapping your fingers at the girl like a naughty puppy, Mr. Rivers, isn't the best way to handle things."

"Brooke." Gran's voice was smooth and calming. "It's time for you to go home. You have school tomorrow."

Suddenly Brooke shot to her feet. "Fine! Whatever. I'll go." She stomped out of the room, past us, and straight to the front door.

Garrett rolled his eyes to the ceiling as Brooke slammed the door behind her. "Again, I apologize for the interruption," he said. "Good night." With a final glare at me, he turned to go.

Gabriella walked out with him and I

followed, but stayed on the porch watching the drama play out in the driveway. Brooke had gotten into the car and had—of course— slammed the passenger door behind her. Garrett hurried down the steps, hopped in his fancy SUV and was clearly having a few words with his reluctant ward as he started up the car.

Gabriella came back up the porch steps. "Poor Garrett," she sighed.

"Poor Garrett?" I scoffed. Any intrigue I *might* have felt for him had winked out at his poor handling of the situation with his ward. "The man is kind of a jerk if you ask me. What's his story?"

"Let me make sure Gran is settled," she said, "and I'll fill you in on the neighbors."

"Okay." I scowled, watching him drive away in his expensive car. Despite the bratty behavior of the girl, I did feel a little sorry for her.

"It's a nice evening," my sister said. "Let's sit out here and talk."

While Gabriella darted inside, I chose one of the big rockers and sat, surveying the condition of the porch. While it was tidy, I wondered over the missing shutter. The sturdy rocking chairs faced out over the property, and off in the distance I could barely make out the silhouette of the neighboring house.

The front door creaked open and I smiled at my sister who'd come out with an open bottle of wine and two glasses. "My hero," I said.

"Here you go." She handed me a glass and poured. "I'll bet you could use this." Gabriella chose the rocker next to me and poured herself a glass. With a soft sigh of her own, she leaned back and took a sip.

"Thank you," I said, and sampled the white wine. "This is good." I glanced over at the bottle she'd stuck in the flowerpot that had held last year's flowers. "What kind of wine is this?"

"It's from a new local winery."

I nodded silently and kept rocking.

Gabriella held up her wine glass as if considering the color. "I couldn't help but notice that you were a tad frazzled meeting Garrett tonight."

I decided not to mention that I'd actually met him earlier at the river. *So much for destiny,* I thought wryly. I took another sip before answering her. "There's just something about him that puts my back up."

"Such as?"

"Pretty much everything." I made a face. "The designer clothes, the Italian shoes, the expensive car, and superior attitude."

"Reminded you of Jared, eh?"

"Not really." My stomach tightened painfully at the mention of my ex. "He doesn't look anything like Jared."

"Garrett Rivers is actually a nice guy once you get to know him," she pointed out.

"He came across as condescending and arrogant to me." *Plus he had those weird eyes...*I thought. *Perhaps that's what made me uneasy.*

"Garrett was upset," Gabriella said. "Brooke has been having problems adjusting to her life here in Illinois."

"From the sound of things, he should try spending some time with her."

"I think Garrett is doing the best he can." She waited a beat. "When did you get to be so judgmental, sis?"

"It's simply not right," I said. "Those who are blessed to have children in their life don't want them...and yet there are other people who would do *anything* to have a child...and can't."

"Hey." Gabriella leaned forward. "I didn't mean to hit on a sore subject."

"You didn't. I was merely thinking out loud."

"I'm sorry Dru. What did the doctors say?" she asked.

"There was never any specific reason why I couldn't conceive. All the medical tests, putting our sex life on a schedule, the stress of hoping every month—that maybe *this* month will be it... There's a humiliation to it all. Fertility counseling put the marriage under a huge strain. And we drifted farther and farther apart. I buried myself in my writing, and Jared...he found other distractions."

Gabriella put her hand on mine. "I'm sorry."

I cleared my throat. "When I found out he was cheating, I confronted him right away. He actually had the audacity to try and rationalize it all by saying that I wasn't woman enough for him. Afterward when Jared's lover ended up getting pregnant—he was quick to insist that the fertility problem *had* to have been mine after all."

"I'm sorry, Dru. That must have hurt."

I sipped some more wine and decided to get everything off my chest. "You know what the worst part of it was?"

"What?" she said softly.

"When he laughed in my face and told me that I'd have to settle for writing stories for everyone else's children—since I wouldn't be having any of my own."

"I think I'm going to call Cammy," Gabriella said thoughtfully.

"How's that?" I said, not following her.

Gabriella sipped her own wine and seemed to consider her options. "I'm going to call our gothic little sister and tell her to bust out all of the occult supplies. Because that rat bastard deserves whatever mo-jo she can throw at him."

Caught off guard, I could only stare.

"Shit." She tossed back the rest of her wine. "I might even want to pitch in and assist, myself."

"Whoa." Her dry comment had me laughing. "Your dark side is showing, Ella."

She put her shoulders back. "The daughters of Midnight are descended from a long line of herbalists, healers and wise—"

"Women," I finished for her. "I know, I know."

"Yeah?" Gabriella raised her eyebrows. "Well, maybe you should act like you *know* it."

"Meaning what?"

"You've drifted so far from your roots, Dru," she said. "I know that you had to be discreet, but you went overboard in the attempt to hide your abilities from Jared."

"You're absolutely right." I nodded in acknowledgment, even as her words caused me to flinch. "It wasn't merely discretion. I abandoned everything Gran taught us, because *blending in* made my life easier. Jared would have only made fun of a wise woman's traditions."

"Well, you don't have to do that anymore," my sister insisted. "I think it's time that you got back to who you truly are, and *not* the woman you thought Jared wanted."

I blew out a tired breath. "I've recently come to understand that myself."

"Take some time and settle in," she suggested. "There's plenty to do around here, and the grounds deserve more attention than I could give them. I did my best, but honestly, the flowers have been sulking since you moved to Chicago. Besides, I think it would do you a world of good."

"Gardening." I tried for a joke. "Cheaper than therapy, and you get flowers."

"Exactly," Gabriella agreed, and tapped her wineglass to mine.

***

The next morning I pulled my hair back in a low ponytail, slapped on some sunscreen, tugged a ball cap over my head and pulled my hair through the back of the hat. Proudly, I slipped on my oldest work boots, jeans, and sweatshirt. Gabriella had managed to find my old brown gardening coat the night before, and I shrugged it on.

"Before supper, those pots on the front porch will all be replanted," I promised, and dropped a kiss on Gran's cheek as she sipped her morning tea.

"Good." She nodded. "I'll want a hand in

planting them too."

"I was thinking pansies," I said, grabbing a bottle of water.

"Perfect." She smiled. "I'd like them all in shades of yellow and blue."

"Great minds think alike," I agreed, and headed outside.

I hauled all of the tools out of the potting shed, loaded up the wheel barrow and rolled the whole business to the front of the house. I stood for a few moments, studying the hedges and remembering all the photos Gran had taken of the three of us every spring, standing in front of those fuzzy hedges holding our Easter baskets.

I tugged on a pair of gardening gloves and attacked that smothering clematis vine first. Within an hour the pussy willow hedges were exposed and standing taller. I raked all of the dried vines into a pile in the middle of the front yard and started exploring the strip of garden that ran adjacent to the front walkway.

Sure enough, daffodils were bent over under a layer of autumn leaves. I pulled off the garden gloves, mentally crossed my fingers that my manicure would hold up and started gently lifting the leaves away from the flowers that were struggling to bloom. Relying on my sense of touch to remove the wet leaves and not do too much damage to the daffodils, I crawled along on my hands and knees, working my way down the long bed. As I'd expected, tulip foliage had broken the ground as well.

"Pink pansies would be charming as an under planting." I studied the uncovered flowers as I knelt in the grass. *Once I'd cleaned up the worst of the front yard, I'd make a run to the nursery and get some,* I thought. Sort of a reward to myself for all the hard work.

Wiping an itch from my nose, I stood and grabbed the rake. Ditching the jacket, I went to work. A half hour later, and I'd managed to work up a good sweat. My shoulders were screaming at me, but I kept working. I knew I'd be sore tomorrow—but I didn't care. My satisfaction grew as the leaf pile did. Clipping the band off the yard waste bags, I snapped one open and started to transfer the dead clematis vines and wet leaves into the long paper bags.

I had a nice row of bags filled when a big, black SUV pulled in our driveway. Leaning on the handle of the rake, I watched as Garrett Rivers stepped out of his car.

Once again, he looked like a million bucks. He'd left a long cloud gray wool coat open, and the collar was popped, which accented his cheekbones. *He probably did that on purpose,* I decided. I could see that he wore a navy turtleneck with trim gray slacks.

He walked toward me with a folder tucked under his arm. There was a determination in his stride, and it took everything I had not to curl my lip.

"Good morning." He came to a stop on the sidewalk opposite of me.

His shoes were Gucci, and spotless. I had to fight the urge to toss a rake full of wet leaves on them. Not wanting to give into the temptation, I let the rake drop to the grass. "Mr. Rivers." I nodded and picked up another yard waste bag.

"I wanted to apologize for last night," he said, tucking his hands in the coat's pockets.

"Oh?" I tilted my head to one side and studied him. An apology was the last thing I'd expected, and it made it hard to hold onto my dislike of the man. *Then again, maybe I could find another reason...* I thought. Especially since he continued to stand there and gawk at me.

"I feel badly that we interrupted your homecoming." He sighed. "I was frustrated and angry at Brooke for running off again. Still, I shouldn't have taken it out on you."

"Gabriella told me that Brooke's been having a tough time." I snapped the yard waste bag open, knelt down, and proceeded to fill the bag with leaves and vines.

He narrowed his eyes as I continued to work. "Your grandmother and sisters have been very kind to Brooke, and to me. I wouldn't want anything to ruin that friendship."

"It won't," I grunted, shoving more leaves in the bag.

"Can I ask what you're doing?" He sounded slightly annoyed as I continued to work.

"Cleaning up the gardens." I spared him a glance. "I'd think that would be fairly obvious."

"With hands like those?"

I checked my grubby hands. The green manicure was still holding up nicely, sparkling in the sunlight. "I try and wear gloves—" I caught myself. *Why was I explaining it to him?* I wondered. "What does it matter?" I said, scowling at him.

"Gabriella mentioned you were an author. I assumed you'd be writing, not doing yard work."

What an insufferable ass, I thought, resting back on my heels. "The women in my family garden. I happen to enjoy both working in the gardens, *and* writing."

"Your sister said you'd be starting another book soon," he said, sounding confused. "Besides, you should truly consider hiring a landscaper for a project of this size."

I bristled. "Why, because I'm female and unable to do manual labor?"

"No, no. That's not what I meant." Garrett shook his head and tried again. "I assumed that you'd need some down time...Gabriella mentioned your break up wasn't amicable."

"My sister says a lot it seems." Embarrassed and sliding towards angry, I struggled to keep my voice pleasant. "I suppose she told you all the sordid details of my divorce as well? How exciting for you."

"No, she didn't, and that comment was beneath you." Mr. Rivers gave me a disapproving stare. "Gabriella would never gossip. She's incredibly proud of your books—and of you."

"Hello Garrett!" Gran's voice stopped me from replying.

"Good morning, Mrs. Midnight." He smiled at my grandmother, and when he did, my stomach dropped to my feet.

Jesus, the man was stunning. I swallowed hard. *And he's annoying and arrogant, as well.* I tuned back in, just in time to hear the end of Gran's sentence.

"...done a wonderful job on the yard?"

"Huh?" I shook my head. "What did you say, Gran?" I started to rise.

"Allow me," he said, courteously taking my elbow and assisting me to my feet.

I resisted the urge to yank away from him. "Thank you," I said, my tone barely polite.

"Drusilla, you should really stop and take a lunch break," Gran called from the doorway.

"Is it lunch time?" I rolled up the final leaf bag and stacked it with the rest. "I'll come inside, Gran, and make you something."

"I'm fine dear. Ella made me lunch earlier." Gran wheeled her walker toward the steps. "But you should eat something, especially after skipping breakfast."

"You did all this and didn't eat anything today?" Garrett checked his watch. "It's 1:30," he said with a frown.

"Really?" I leaned over to see the time for myself. Without thinking about it, I reached for his wrist and tugged it closer. "Huh." My breath huffed out. "I didn't realize how much time had passed."

Silently, his strange eyes flashed to mine.

I wasn't sure if I'd offended him by looking at his precious Rolex, or if he was worried that I'd muss his expensive coat with my grubby fingers. "Sorry," I said, dropping his wrist and easing out of his personal space.

He visibly exhaled as I moved back.

I guess Mr. Rivers didn't appreciate the honest smell of wet leaves, sweat, and dirt? Instead of sneering at him, I focused on my grandmother. "I was going to make a nursery run, Gran, and go get those pansies I'd promised you. I'll stop for a burger on the way."

"Good." She inclined her head. "Garrett, are those the files for Gabriella?"

At her words, Garrett remembered them. "Yes," he said, taking them to my grandmother. "I wanted to tell her that we approve of the design and we're ready to launch on the proposed date."

That was the reason he was worried about hard feelings. My sister must be designing a website for him.

"She's upstairs working in her office." Gran said. "She'll be happy to talk to you about them."

He nodded and went straight up the front steps. Courteously, he held the door open for my grandmother and followed her in the house without another word to me.

I shrugged it off and decided now was as good a time as any for a lunch break. I glanced at the daffodils that stood noticeably taller along the front walkway. As I studied them, a pair at my feet quivered and popped up perfectly straight.

"Chivalry, eh?" I chuckled to the daffodils. I hunkered down and addressed the flowers. "You think so?" In answer, another duo of daffodils popped up straighter. I narrowed my eyes and considered the man who'd managed to annoy me twice in such a short amount of time. "It's been a long time since any flowers talked to me. I appreciate the message."

A pair of robins landed in the strip of flower bed a few feet away and started to dig for worms. They chirped back and forth, even as I ran my fingers over the sunny yellow trumpets. "I'll bring you back some company this afternoon," I promised the daffodils. "Then you'll have someone else to talk to—besides me."

CHAPTER FOUR

I retrieved my wallet and the keys for the family's old pickup truck and was cruising down the Great River Road toward Alton shortly thereafter. The sun shining off the Mississippi River had me smiling, and I cranked the radio up and enjoyed my drive.

I hit a drive-thru in Alton and stopped only long enough to eat a burger and fries, but afterward, I wasn't impressed with any of the big hardware store's selections of annuals. I called Gran on my way back to the village and asked her if there was anywhere else in the area I could try. She recommended a place I'd never heard of, *River Road Garden Center.*

"Your sister is friends with the owner, Max," Gran said.

After disconnecting the call, I followed her directions and pulled into a pretty garden center twenty minutes later. Taking my soft drink with me, I eased down to the gravel parking lot and started exploring. While the nursery wasn't large, it was impressive none-the-less. Pretty displays of spring blooming shrubs and annuals were set near the front porch of the building. Large wooden tables held a myriad of colorful, cold-tolerant pansies and violas. A few greenhouses were situated off to the left, and I could make out masses of plants, waiting for warmer weather, to be sold.

Delighted by what I saw, I snagged a big cart and headed for the nearby tables of pansies. Within five minutes I had a flat of blue and yellow violas set aside for the cobalt containers on Gran's front porch. I spotted some trailing ivy and picked out a few small cell packs to add to the pots.

The breeze was shifting back to chilly, but I didn't care. Comfortable and content, I soaked up the vibes from the flowers. "Heart's ease," I murmured the wise woman's name for the flower.

Perhaps I had been overly sensitive to Garrett River's comments, I considered my reaction as I shopped. I was honest enough to admit that I'd been annoyed at his assumption that I was unable to take care of the gardens myself; and I'd been mortified at the thought of Gabriella sharing personal information about my divorce with him. *After all, he might be friendly with my family, but the man was still a stranger to me.* As I mulled over the situation, the perky flowers brushed against my fingertips.

"Happy thoughts," I chuckled at their hidden message, and sipped at the last of my soda. The flowers were working their magick for me like they had for most of my life. Feeling a bit more settled, I returned my attention back to choosing the best purple and pink pansies for the garden, and a shadow fell across me.

"Hello, again," said a familiar voice.

I snapped my head up and discovered none other than Garrett Rivers standing on the opposite side of the pansy tables. "Hello." I managed to nod politely, even as he studied me with those spooky eyes.

He tucked his hands in his coat pockets. "I thought I'd find you here."

In a village the size of Ames Crossing, the odds of running into your neighbors were pretty high. The daffodils at home had declared that he was in fact, *chivalrous*...and I reminded myself that holding onto a grudge on such a pretty spring day was pointless. Especially since I hadn't exactly been at my best either. I pulled the bill of my cap back so I could see his entire face. "Are you following me, Mr. Rivers?" I asked.

"No." He blinked at my comment. "I have an appointment for a landscaping consultation."

"Sure..." I narrowed one eye at him. "That's what they all say."

"I do have an appointment with the owner," he explained, appearing completely out of place in his elegant clothes.

"Umm hmm..." Selecting another six pack of rosy-colored pansies, I held the flowers up to consider their white and purple faces.

"Actually, I prefer to work with local business and contractors whenever possible," he explained.

I placed the six pack in my cart and shifted my eyes to his face. "Stalker," I said, deadpan.

I could see the exact moment he figured out that I'd been teasing him, and when it hit home, his grin was lightning fast. My stomach gave a flutter in reaction, and I told myself to ignore it.

Hadn't I already decided that Garrett Rivers was absolutely *not* my type?

"Is this guy hassling you, Miss?" came a new male voice. I shifted and had to look way up to see a buff, blonde man who stood with his arms folded across his chest. His stern tone of voice conveyed one thing, but the grin on his face told a different story.

"I'm fine," I was quick to say.

"Hello, Max," Garrett stuck out a hand to shake.

Max. This must be the owner, I thought.

"Garrett." Max reached out and shook his hand. Like me, the man was wearing sturdy work clothes and a ball cap. "How're things going?" He clapped Garrett on the shoulder.

"Fine." Garrett nodded.

"Heard Brooke made a run for it again." Max's brown eyes twinkled.

Garrett sighed. "She got as far as the Midnight's gardens."

"She still badgering you to let her have a kitten?"

While Garrett muttered over that, I considered the men. Clearly, Max knew not only Garrett, he was familiar with my family as well.

"Hello, Max. I'm Dru." I introduced myself. "My grandmother, Priscilla Midnight, suggested I should stop by."

"Hey Dru." Max's smile was endearing. His hand gripped mine with a casual strength. "Gabriella told me you were moving back home and tackling the gardens. How's your grandmother doing today?"

"Fine," I said casually, even while I balked at hearing the words *Gabriella told me*, again. I told myself not to feel embarrassed. "I promised Gran I'd replant the containers on the porch today."

Max shifted his gaze to the cart. "The cobalt blue ceramic ones?"

"Exactly." I nodded.

"The blue and yellow colors are going to be

great in there," he said.

I smiled. Here was someone I could be comfortable with. A nice, hard working man who knew his plants. "I'm going to add the ivy to trail down the sides."

"I have some white alyssum, hardened off," Max said. "That would be nice mixed in with the violas."

"Really?" I asked. "Where?"

Max pointed out some tables along the south side of the first greenhouse. "Want me to walk you over there?"

"No, that's okay," I assured him.

"Jesse is inside if you need anything else, or when you're ready to check out," Max said.

I grabbed the handle of the cart and started forward. "Thank you, Max."

I wandered the garden center and deliberated over the changes to the community since I'd been gone...and the additions to it. Mr. Rivers and Max were complete opposites, and I would have never imagined Garrett as being friendly with a down-to-earth man like Max.

Or maybe you're still measuring all men against your ex, I chastised myself.

I added some fragrant alyssum to my other selections, noted the sale price for potting mix, and decided to buy a couple bags. Wheeling the cart forward, it was easy to see that the store had started its life out as a small house. Now, the front rooms were a check out area that boasted a clever display of houseplants, summer bulbs, and hand tools. Farther off to the side, soil additives, fertilizer, shovels, hoes, and rakes were arranged.

I could see Max behind a desk through an open doorway, and Garrett was sitting opposite him, going over what had to be landscaping plans.

"Do you have any snapdragons hardened off and ready to plant?" I asked the young man behind the counter. He had a name tag pinned on his jacket, announcing him to be Jesse.

Jesse checked a clipboard. "Those should be ready in the next two to three weeks."

"Thank you," I put away my wallet. "I'll definitely come back and get some."

Jesse picked up two twenty-five pound bags of potting soil and followed me outside. He tossed them in the open bed of the old truck.

"Want some help loading the flowers in your car?" Jesse asked.

"No, I've got it." With a smile, I waved him away and arranged the flats in the truck bed against the tailgate.

***

I planted the two flats of pink and purple pansies first. Seeing those bright sassy faces under the daffodils and around the tulip greenery made me ridiculously happy. Revved up, I dumped the old potting mix in the wheelbarrow so the containers would be ready for the fresh soil I'd purchased. Whistling to myself, I added the old soil to the compost pile in the back and loaded up a couple bags of mulch from the shed, for the return trip to the front. Carefully, I mulched around the daffodils, pansies, and emerging tulips.

By the time I lugged all the yard waste bags to the end of the driveway to be picked up, I was filthy and completely content. I brushed my gloved hands off as I considered the changes to the yard. The difference I'd made in one day's work was enormous. There was still plenty of work to be done...the boxwood hedges needed a hard trim, and there were a few more perennial beds that needed to be cleaned out...but already things looked better.

Gran came out before dinner and helped me plant up the pots on the porch. She sat in a chair working on one, while I knelt beside her finishing the second.

"What did you think of the new garden center?" Gran asked.

"It was a great place." I patted the last of my violas down in fresh potting soil.

"And what did you think of Max Dubois?"

"He seemed like he knew what he was doing. I'm excited about going back to the nursery again for more plants, when it gets warmer."

My sister poked her head out the front door. "The chicken and dumplings will be ready in twenty minutes."

"Perfect," I said to her. "I'm starving."

Gran competently tucked some trailing ivy at the outside edge of her container. "These are a nice choice, Drusilla. The ivy vine symbolizes fidelity."

"I remember," I said. "That's why brides use it in their bouquets." *Too bad I hadn't had a bouquet when Jared and I ran off and eloped...* I brushed aside the thought and smiled at my grandmother instead. "I like how the ivy spills over the sides."

"Just so." Gran nodded her head. "Max is attractive, don't you think, Drusilla?"

I slanted my eyes over at the shift in topics and wondered what she was up to. "Sure."

Gran added another viola to her pot. "Ella thinks Max is handsome."

"Very funny, Gran," she said, walking over to see the progress on the flower pots.

I brushed the soil from my fingers. "And Garrett Rivers?" I asked my sister. "What do you think of him?"

"Garrett is a client, and Max and I are good friends, nothing more."

Gran glanced over her shoulder. "You could change that dynamic with Max anytime that you wish, sweetheart."

"Max and his fiancée broke up last year," Gabriella said. "He hasn't seen anyone romantically since then...I don't think he's ready."

I tilted my head and thought it over. I could kind of see my sister being interested in Max, the nurseryman. "And you'd know that because you're *just* his friend."

She puckered up. "I know that because he confided in me as a friend."

"Well," I began, keeping a careful eye on her face, "if you're not interested in him romantically, maybe *I* could be." I tucked my tongue in my cheek. "That was some serious eye candy. I'll bet there's plenty of wonderful muscles under that flannel shirt..."

She glared.

I began to chuckle. "Ella, you're still way too easy to get a rise out of."

"You shouldn't talk about him that way." My sister stuck her nose in the air and went back in the house. When the storm door slapped shut behind her, my grandmother started to snicker.

I picked up the empty cell packs. "Don't think I don't know that you set that whole exchange up, Gran."

My grandmother fluffed the ivy she'd planted. "Gabriella's carried a torch for Max for almost two years."

"Really?" I asked as I finished cleaning up. "What in the world is she waiting for?"

"Maybe you should ask her," Gran said.

***

I woke early the next morning to misery. It felt like every muscle in my body was screaming at me. I rolled out of bed in my oversized, faded nightshirt, tried to stretch my arms over my head, and winced. I grabbed a pair of aqua fuzzy socks for my feet, but because of the stiff muscles, it took me twice as long to get them on. Finally, I shuffled across the hall to brush my teeth before heading downstairs for a very large cup of tea and some ibuprofen.

I staggered into the kitchen and almost walked right into a broad, muscular back covered in denim.

"Morning." Max Dubois stood in my family's kitchen, grinning at me.

"Sonofa—" I cut myself off in mid swear. There was no help for it now. The man was seeing me with bed hair and in my pajamas. I squinted up at him. "Max."

"Hey Dru." He stayed where he was, sipping from a large mug.

I tried to step around him, and he moved the same way. I tried again, and we ended up blocking each other. I was torn between laughing and annoyance. "Max, don't make me hurt you," I warned him. "I'm in desperate need of ibuprofen and caffeine."

Max stepped back, and I managed to get to the cupboards. To my infinite relief the medicine was still stored in the same place. Gabriella hovered at the stove, scrambling a large pan of eggs.

"Morning," she said, and handed me a glass of juice. "Do you want some breakfast?"

"Please," I managed, and took the pills.

"Scrambled eggs okay?" she asked.

"Don't make me beg." I went to the table with my juice and eased down into a chair with a groan.

I heard the approaching thump of Gran's walker before she spoke. "I warned you not to overdo it yesterday."

"Yes, you did," I muttered. "I'll be fine once I get moving."

To my surprise, Max began setting the table. I watched as he went to the correct drawer and pulled out flatware. He bustled around, working in tandem with Gabriella. When the toast popped up she put it on a plate and passed it to him. Max placed the plate on the center of the table and added the butter and a jar of preserves to the side.

He had Gran's chair pulled out for her before I could blink, and he competently wheeled the walker out of the way once she was settled.

Gabriella switched off the heat under the eggs, and Max brought a tea kettle to the table, setting it on a trivet. He took his seat beside me, and it was all so smooth that I realized this was an old routine for them.

I sipped at my juice and wondered at the easy familiarity between Max and my family. I was opening my mouth to ask about it when my sister spoke up.

"It's Wednesday," she said, as if that explained everything.

"I'm sorry?" I set my juice glass down.

"On Wednesdays, Max comes by for breakfast." Gabriella scooped out some eggs and put them on my plate.

"Oh," I said.

"This past winter, every Wednesday morning Max would help your sister get me in the car for my physical therapy appointments." Gran helped herself to the toast.

"I was happy to help," Max said.

"Fixing breakfast for you was the least I could do." Gabriella served the eggs and took a seat.

"Besides," Max said, "this way I get to spend the morning with my two favorite girls."

Gabriella blushed at the compliment, and I was finally alert enough to notice that my sister was wearing a nice purple sweater, jeans, *and* makeup. In fact, she looked great. I had a very female moment to regret the state of my old, faded night shirt. Not to mention my hair still being in the messy braid I'd slept in. However, from the relaxed vibes Max was putting off, it was hard to hold onto any embarrassment for too long.

While Max and Gabriella carried on an

animated conversation about her updating his garden center's website for the spring season, my grandmother kicked me under the table. I nudged her back and realized that my sister wasn't simply crushing on Max Dubois.

She was, in fact, head over heels in love with him.

CHAPTER FIVE

I managed five more days working in the gardens before a series of storms rolled in. I stood in the living room, scowling out the window on a gloomy Monday morning, watching the rain fall.

"April showers..." I told myself the flowers deserved a good soaking, but I wondered what I would do to keep myself busy today. Gran had gone off with her friends into Alton for lunch and the movies. Shadow perched on the back of the sofa, intermittently glaring at either the rain or me. The cat was still suspicious of my presence in the house. I gave him a wide berth and decided to go hunt up Gabriella.

I found my sister working away in her little office upstairs in the attic. The unfinished walls should have looked bleak, but instead they were rustic and charming. To add to the ambiance, she had strung multi-colored faery lights across the ceiling, and her chunky wooden desk was exactly right tucked against the window. An old faded rug covered most of her work space floor, and an industrial floor lamp by her desk brightened up the whole corner.

She had headphones on and was nodding in time to whatever music she was listening to. I saw a long bookshelf on one wall filled with books. Above that, a dozen different book covers were blown up and pinned on the slanted walls. My lips twitched as I admired the covers. They were stunning, dark and sexy... and unless I missed my guess, the covers were for romance novels, and probably erotica.

I caught a glimpse of her computer screen, and discovered she was working with a photo shop program. As I watched, she dropped the title of the book in place. I glanced back at the art on the walls and it clicked. "Hey Sis," I said, and she didn't respond in any way. "Ella," I repeated, dropping my hand on her shoulder.

Gabriella jumped about a foot straight up in

the air. "Dru!" She yanked the headphones off.

"Oh god, I'm sorry." I gave her shoulder a squeeze. "I got rained out from gardening and was bored. I didn't mean to startle you."

With a light laugh, she patted her chest. "I was caught up and not paying attention."

"I didn't know you were designing romance novel covers these days. I leaned over her shoulder and studied what she was working on. "Ella, I'm impressed. This is fabulous!"

She leaned back in her chair. "It has a way to go before I'd consider it fabulous, but thanks."

I went over for a closer inspection of the artwork pinned to the walls. "I had no idea. When did you start doing this?"

"I branched out last year with a local INDY author. She liked the cover so much she gave my name to a couple of colleagues of hers, and now it's a nice supplement to my income."

I plucked a book at random from the bookshelf and noticed it matched up to my sister's art on the wall. "Mind if I read this?"

"Sure, you'll like that one. Now I don't want to be rude, but I have a bunch of work to do."

"Okay," I said. "I'll get out of your hair.

Thanks."

She slid the earphones back on. "I'll catch you later."

I read for a few hours until the rain turned to drizzle. The book was a fun romp, and I enjoyed the writer's sense of humor. After being outside for the past few days, I was feeling somewhat hemmed in. I checked out the window and set the book aside. *What I needed,* I decided, *was a project.* Since I couldn't work outside in the gardens, maybe I'd tackle the reorganization of the potting shed instead. After all, if I was going to be sharing it with the cat and her brood, I should probably make it safer.

I found my boots, snagged an old beach towel from the rag bin, and put it in a large garbage bag. Grabbing bundles of dried lavender, sage and rosemary from the kitchen, I scouted up some cleaning supplies. Once I had everything together, I tugged the hood of my raincoat over my head and made a run for the shed across the back yard. I ducked inside, and Mama cat came out with her brood. I gave Mama a bit of attention and pulled a wooden crate down from where it had been stored in the rafters overhead.

I worked around the curious kittens easily enough. I hung the big bundles of herbs from the rafters, and the fragrance immediately helped ward off the mustiness. Pulling on a pair of work gloves, I swept the place out, and then mercilessly cleaned and reorganized the potting bench to my preferences. I scrubbed the glass in the windows, threw away old broken tools, and removed any clutter that couldn't be reused.

Next, I restacked terra cotta pots on one end and organized all the empty hanging baskets and window boxes. Kneeling down, I cleared off the wide bottom shelf, placing the big wooden crate to one side. I folded the old towel, placed it on the bottom, and picked up the first nearby kitten and put him or her inside the box.

A white and orange head popped up over the edge a moment later. With *meeping* sounds the kitten called to its mother, and Mama cat hopped in the crate and the rest of the kittens were quick to follow her. "Happy home," I said to Mama cat. "That should be better for your family."

I put the old mashed cardboard box in the garbage bag and was opening the door, intending to take the garbage out, when I bounced off of Brooke James.

"Whoa!" I automatically reached to steady the girl before she ended up on her backside in a puddle.

She yanked away from me hard enough that she hit her shoulder on the frame of the door. "Don't touch me!"

I held my hands up. "Easy, Brooke. I'm not going to hurt you." Behind her back, tendrils of the sorcerer's violet stretched out protectively towards her.

She glared. "I came to see the kittens."

"I see." I tipped my head to one side and considered the situation. *The girl should be in school. What on earth was she doing here before noon on a school day?* I stepped back to allow her to enter the potting shed anyway.

Brooke stepped inside, and the vines with their purple star shaped flowers dropped back in place. When she brushed past me I noticed three things. One: she reeked of cigarette smoke. Two: she was soaking wet, and three: a bruise was starting to form under her right eye. My stomach gave a hard jerk. I checked her knuckles, and they were unmarked. It took me a moment, but I managed to speak calmly. "Did you get into a fight at school?"

Her head whipped around. "No. Why would you think that?"

"Cause Middle School is hell on earth, and you have a nice mouse, right there." I tapped a finger under my own eye.

"Mouse?" she frowned.

"The starting of a shiner," I tried to explain, and when she continued to stare at me like I was speaking a foreign language, I tried again. "You're getting a black eye." I finally said.

"Shit," she hissed the word out and I tried not to laugh.

I folded my arms and leaned against the door. "Want to tell me what happened?"

Brooke held her right hand defensively close to her chest. "Why do you care?" It was clear that she expected me to launch into a lecture.

I decided the situation called for a little humor. I pulled over an old lawn chair, opened it, and sat. "When I was in Middle School, I got in a fight once. Maryjane Turner had shoved me into a row of garbage cans in the lunchroom. She'd tried to take my lunch money." I leaned back in my chair and considered the girl as she stood there shivering from the damp and the cold.

"Whatever." Brooke curled her lip.

"Well, Maryjane was a bully," I continued. "No doubt about it, and she'd been picking on me all year. But that day, I sort of snapped."

"*Pfft.*" Brooke rolled her eyes. "What did you do, pull her hair?"

"Not quite..." I shook my head. "First, I got up from the floor and wiped the lime jello off my shirt."

Brooke sniffed. "And then?"

"I grabbed the first thing I could find, which was a lunch tray, and I..." I paused for dramatic effect.

"*And?*" Brooke demanded.

"Well I'm not proud of myself, but Maryjane had it coming."

"What did you do?" Brooke wanted to know.

"I hit her in the face with that lunch tray as hard as I could."

Brooke stared at me.

"It took three teachers to pull us apart." I reminisced. "To be honest, while we rolled around on the cafeteria floor screaming and punching each other, there *may* have been some hair pulling. I got a three-day suspension for fighting and my grandparents grounded me for a month."

"Was it worth it?" Brooke asked.

I smiled. "It certainly was. Maryjane and all her mean-girl friends stayed well away from me after that."

The kittens climbed out of the crate and made a beeline for Brooke. "I'm going to go inside and eat some lunch," I said, standing up. "If you need anything, you know where to find me. Otherwise, be sure and shut the door when you leave." I picked up the garbage bag and let myself out. She flinched as I passed her, but otherwise was silent.

I'd been inside the house worrying over her for maybe five minutes when the backdoor opened with a soft creak. I leaned against the counter and studied the girl who hovered halfway in the kitchen door. "Gabriella's working in her office and Gran's out for the day." I waited a beat. "No one knows you're here. In case you wondered."

"Okay." Brooke came all the way in. She was still keeping her right hand protectively close to her chest.

I walked over to the laundry room off the kitchen and snagged a hoodie and a pair of clean sweats from a folded stack of clothes. I tossed them to her. "These will be too big for you, but at least they're dry."

Brooke caught the sweat pants with her left hand. "Okay," she said again.

"You can change in the powder room if you like."

Brooke nodded and went to do so. I stayed where I was and deliberated over what to do next. I considered calling Garrett Rivers...but the girl was clearly miserable. Maybe I could stall for a while. I went to the freezer and pulled out a big frozen pizza. I had the oven on pre-heat when Brooke came back to the kitchen. She was barefoot and carrying her wet clothes and navy uniform blazer.

"What should I do with them?" Brooke

asked.

"Go ahead and toss everything but the blazer in the dryer." I hooked a thumb towards the laundry room.

"Me?" Brooke's eyes went big from surprise. "Do laundry?"

"You've never done laundry before?" I guessed.

"Of course not." She held the clothes out.

"That blazer is wool," I said, eyeballing it. "Hang it on a plastic hanger and let it drip dry. Everything else can go in the dryer. Choose 'low heat' and set the timer for thirty minutes."

"You expect *me* to do it?"

I raised my eyebrows. "Unless you don't think your smart enough to figure out the dryer by yourself."

Brooke set her jaw and stomped across the kitchen to the laundry room. I waited and heard the sound of the dryer turning on. The rattle of hangers came next, and I slid the pizza out of the box as she came back in the kitchen.

"Did you take the cigarettes out of your jacket pocket?" I asked conversationally.

Brooke jumped guiltily.

"They're probably soaked. I hope you threw them away."

"How did you know?" she asked.

"I smelled the smoke on you."

"You did?"

I tapped a finger to the side of my nose. "The nose knows."

"Can I borrow some socks?" Brooke suddenly asked.

I glanced down at her feet. "Sure, there's some fuzzy socks on top of the dryer. They're Ella's, but she won't mind."

Brooke nodded, went to go fetch a pair, and came back. "Why do you call Gabriella, Ella?"

"It's a nick name. Sometimes, I call Camilla, *Cammy*—and they both call me Dru."

I heard my sister come clambering down the back stairs. She swung into the kitchen and came up short when she spotted the girl. "Brooke, what happened?"

"Brooke's going to borrow some socks," I said, giving my sister a significant look. "Her clothes are all wet."

"I see." Gabriella cleared her throat. "Are you staying for lunch, Brooke?"

Brooke swung her eyes from my sister and back to me. "I guess."

"Why don't you take a—"

"Put some plates on the table." I pointed to the cabinet. "You can manage that. Can't you, Brooke?"

"Yes," she said and went to the cabinet I'd pointed out.

When Brooke turned her back, Gabriella pointed to her own eye. She'd noticed the bruise too.

I nodded in acknowledgment and watched our guest. She still wasn't using her right hand. Not at all. "Ella," I said, casually. "Why don't you get us some soda?"

"Sure." She went to the fridge for three cans.

"I'm not allowed to have soft drinks," Brooke blurted out.

Gabriella handed her a can. "Well, today's your lucky day."

A ghost of a smile hovered on Brooke's face.

"An occasional soda won't hurt you." I reached in the freezer for some ice cubes and wrapped them in a clean tea towel. "We won't say anything if you don't."

"Thanks," Brooke sniffled.

"While we wait for the pizza to bake, you might want to use this on that eye." I handed Brooke the homemade ice pack.

Brooke took the ice pack in her left hand and sat in a kitchen chair. She held the ice to her eye which was getting darker by the minute. "Ouch," she hissed.

"That's a hell of a shiner," I said. "It's going to hurt."

Ella joined her at the table. "What happened, Brooke?" she asked gently.

Brooke sat there sulking and looking miserable. "Clementine Bryant and a few other girls cornered me in the restroom."

"What did they do?" I asked.

"They called me names, and started shoving me." Brooke took the ice away from her eye and stared at the table top. "I tried to stay up, but they kept shoving and I fell down. I guess that's how I hurt my wrist."

"Who hit you?" Ella asked.

"Nobody," Brooke said. "I hit my face on the sink when I fell, that's how I ended up on the floor."

My sister winced at Brooke's words. "Oh, sweetie."

"Well, they might have managed to knock you down, but I'll bet you got back up," I said, gauging the girl.

"Yeah, I did." Brooke's expression was fierce. "They all stood there laughing at me. I was still stuck in the corner...and I swung my book bag as hard as I could, and smacked Clementine right in her stupid face."

"Atta girl," I said, taking the chair beside her. We all sat quietly for a bit. I truly wanted to see how badly she was injured but didn't think she'd allow it.

My sister beat me to it and simply reached for Brooke's hand. "May I see your wrist?"

With a nod, Brooke slowly extended her arm. Ella grazed her fingers across the girl's wrist. Brooke gasped, the color draining from her face.

"Can you wiggle your fingers?" I asked.

"It hurts." Brooke's voice was breathy.

"Might be broken," Ella said, meeting my eyes.

I nodded. "We need to get her to the

Emergency Room."

"I'm going to stabilize your arm and make you a sling," Ella told her. "Sit quietly now."

I reached out and cautiously patted Brooke's left shoulder while my sister bustled around gathering first aid supplies.

"Garrett's going to be really angry at me," Brooke gritted out.

"Don't you worry about that," I said. "You leave him to me."

"I'm scared," Brooke admitted, and then she laid her head down on the kitchen table and cried.

"It's alright," I ran my hand down her bright red hair. "Go ahead and cry, you've had a pretty awful day."

The damn had broken apparently, and Brooke let loose and wailed. I stood, waiting her out, and continued to gently stroke her hair. Shadow the cat came bouncing in the kitchen and hopped from the floor to the chair, and walked across the table to head butt the crying child. He stayed there waiting and watching over her.

When she finally wound down, I plucked a

few paper napkins from the table and handed them to her.

Brooke wiped up her face and blew her nose. "Sorry," she said.

"For what?" I held out my hand for the napkins and when she handed them over, I tossed them in the garbage can.

"For bawling like a baby." Her breath shuddered out, and new tears spilled over.

"Don't be ridiculous." I wiped her face myself. "You don't think that in a house of four females, there hasn't been a few tears shed?"

"I guess," she said, hiccupping a little. Shadow head-butted her again and Brooke reached out to pet the cat.

"Meow." Shadow leaned in closer for a nuzzle.

"We've got you." I promised. "The daughters of Midnight watch out for their own."

"But I'm *not* yours," she whispered, and her bottom lip began to tremble. "I'm not anybody's. Not anymore."

I bent over and took hold of her chin. "You're in our home aren't you?" I lifted my hand until our eyes met. "You came here for help, and like it or not, Brooke, you're getting it."

Her large eyes swam with more tears. "Okay."

I followed my instincts and dropped a gentle kiss on her forehead. "You're not alone. I won't let you down, sweetheart."

CHAPTER SIX

Gabriella stabilized Brooke's injury by loosely rolling a magazine into a tube around the girl's forearm and hand. She tied the magazine closed and used a big scarf to fashion a sling. We loaded her in the car and headed to Alton and the nearest emergency room.

Since my sister had Garrett's phone number, I used her phone to call him. It went straight to voice mail. With an impatient growl, I left a brief message "Garrett, this is Drusilla Midnight. Brooke's hurt her wrist. We're taking her to the hospital in Alton. Call back when you get the message."

I tried again a few more times when we had Brooke admitted to the ER, but everything went to voice mail. After about a half hour, they came to take her in to X-ray.

I tried again after they wheeled the girl off, hissed in impatience, and left my fourth terse message. "Damn it. He's still not answering."

"Keeps going straight to voice mail?" Gabriella guessed.

"Yes." I disconnected. "Should we call Max?" I asked her. "I got the impression they were friends."

She sat up straight in her chair. "That's a good idea. Call Max now."

I selected Max from her contacts, he answered immediately. "Hi Ella," he said cheerfully.

"Max, it's Dru. Listen, we're at the hospital —" I began.

"Is Ella alright?" he asked so quickly that I blinked at the phone. I resisted the urge to smirk at my sister. *Sure, you two are just friends...* "She's fine," I said. "It's Brooke. She might have broken her wrist, and we can't locate Garrett."

Max promised to track Garrett down, and he hung up.

Where was the man? I wondered. *Brooke*

was hurt and he was no where to be found?

When Gabriella's cell phone rang five minutes later, I saw it was Max and simply handed her the phone.

I fretted and tried to sit still while we waited for Brooke to return. When I heard the quick rap of shoes on the tile floor I swung my head around, and Garrett Rivers came hustling into the treatment room. "Where is she?" he asked as soon as he saw me.

"They took her off for an X-ray," my sister said.

"How bad is it? I want to speak to her doctor."

"Let me go tell the nurse that you've arrived." Gabriella ducked out.

Garrett stalked across the room. "What a day! First the meetings with the chamber of commerce go all to hell, I get your message, then I was stuck in traffic, and you're blowing up my damn phone the entire time..."

"Maybe you should try *answering* the damn phone," I snapped. "Or are you too important to be bothered with sending a text message?"

He yanked his phone out of his coat pocket

and slammed it on the counter. "My phone is acting up! It wouldn't let me make any outgoing calls, or even send a text! As soon as I got your first message I dropped everything and drove straight here."

Caught off guard by his reaction and the phone that had cracked from the impact, I reevaluated the man in front of me. "Sorry," I said cautiously. "That would be frustrating."

"What happened?" he asked. "Did the school call you when they couldn't contact me? How did she get hurt, was it during gym cl—"

"Garrett." I held up a hand to silence him. "I think you better sit down. There's a few things you should know before Brooke gets back."

***

They say people can smolder with rage, or maybe the better term would be *seethe*. I'd never really seen it before. But when I told him how Brooke had come to be injured, Garrett Rivers, who was sitting perfectly still in the bedside chair of the treatment room, was in fact, seething.

His eyes had an intensity that made me want to back up several paces, and to my surprise he switched it off immediately when Brooke was wheeled back into the treatment room.

"Brooke." He stood and waited for the orderly to maneuver the bed back in place. It had barely come to a stop before Garrett bent over and awkwardly dropped a kiss on the top of her head. "You scared me." He blew out a long breath.

"You're here." Brooke sounded surprised, and that made my heart ache.

"Of course I'm here." He took her chin in his hand and tipped her face up. "Damn, honey." He winced over the black eye.

"Dru said it's a 'hell of a shiner'," Brooke quoted proudly.

"Yes it is." His lips bowed up slightly.

Impressed that the girl had allowed any sort of physical contact, and that Garrett really seemed to be trying with her, I eased back. "I'll give you two some privacy."

"No!" Brooke's eyes shot to my face. "Please don't leave. Stay."

I patted her foot. "I can stay," I said, briskly.

"Don't you worry."

"I'm not worried," Brooke said. "You promised me a pizza."

"After the Doctor checks you out and says it's okay. I'll get you a pizza bigger than your head," I promised.

Brooke leaned her head back against the pillow. "*And* a Dr. Pepper."

"No soft drinks," Garrett argued.

"Jumbo sized," I promised her, then I shut my mouth as the ER doctor came in with the results of the X-ray.

***

Brooke had broken her wrist. A greenstick fracture, they called it. She'd been fitted with a plastic temporary cast—a sort of wrist brace, and had been sent home. My promise of pizza had been vetoed by Garrett, and he'd whisked the girl off with a terse thank you to my sister and me.

I hadn't seen either Garrett or Brooke since that day, and I wondered how the girl was doing. A week had passed since we'd taken

Brooke to the ER, and I'd told myself I was relieved at the chance for some peace and quiet and used the time working on the gardens in the back of the property.

Today, since there was no wind, I decided to burn all the plant material and twigs I'd cleared from the beds. The sun was shining and the temperatures hovered in the low 50's. Dressed in a ratty purple sweatshirt, old jeans and sturdy boots, I hauled another big pile to the backyard fire pit. I added an armful to the flames and stood back while they caught.

While the dead foliage burned, I started to sweep off the brick patio area adjacent to my potting shed. I'd pulled the quartet of Adirondack chairs out of the garage and had scrubbed them down the day before.

After the past few weeks of mercilessly cutting back the spent foliage and cleaning out the flower beds, the gardens were doing much better, and perennials had started to pop up all around the property. In the shade of our old oak tree, hostas were pushing up taller every day. The painted ferns were unfurling, and the bleeding heart that had managed to survive tucked against the potting shed was filled with dangling heart shaped blossoms of pink.

I added more sticks and dead weeds to the fire and calculated the risks of planting up a few baskets and containers with other annuals. We were barely past the freeze date, but my instincts said it would be safe to plant annuals. "Worse case scenario," I said to myself, giving the fire a poke, "I could always store the baskets in the shed if night time temperatures dipped back below freezing."

"Hey, Dru." Gabriella's voice snapped me back to the here and now. "Look who's here."

I turned around to find Brooke James standing besides my sister. Her black eye had faded to a pale purple and green. She was casually dressed in jeans, tennis shoes and a sweatshirt. A hot pink plaster cast was now on the girl's right arm, and the shirt's long sleeve had been cut to accommodate it.

"Hi Brooke." I pushed my ball cap back. "How are you feeling?"

"Better," she said, and nervously cleared her throat.

Gabriella patted the girl's shoulder. "Garrett

came by with notes for his website and brought Brooke to see us."

I scanned the backyard. Apparently, Mr. Rivers hadn't deigned to come outdoors. "That's nice," was the safest comment I could make.

"I wanted to thank you both for helping me last week." Her words were stiff and obviously rehearsed.

"You're welcome," I said, and added another batch of clippings to the fire.

"I'm glad you came to see us today," Gabriella said kindly.

"What are you doing?" Brooke asked me.

"Burning off the dead clippings and twigs from the garden." I gave the fire a jab with the metal poker.

"Can I help?" she asked, and I don't know who was more surprised. Her or me.

"Maybe you should sit and rest," Gabriella suggested.

"I've been stuck inside for a week," Brooke complained.

"Sure," I said. "You can help." I handed her a bundle of twigs. "Toss those in."

"Really?" Brooke almost smiled. "I can?"

"Be careful," my sister warned as Brooke flung the twigs in from a safe distance.

"I've got this, Ella," I promised. "You can go back inside and have your meeting. Brooke can keep me company."

I waited to speak until my sister had gone back in the house. "Have you gone back to school yet?" I asked the girl.

"No." She shook her head. "Tomorrow, he's making me go back."

I handed her the poker. "Give the branches a shove, that way I can add more."

"Okay." Brooke caught her tongue between her teeth and concentrated on her task, while I scooped up the last of the burn pile and dropped it in the fire pit.

"Step back," I warned her. "It's going to catch quickly." With snaps and pops the fire roared to life.

"Wicked," Brooke murmured.

"Do you mind keeping an eye on that, so I can finish sweeping up?" I asked casually.

"I can," Brooke said, way too seriously.

While Brooke gave the fire an occasional

poke, I couldn't decide if the pleased expression on her face from being given something to do—was adorable—or unbearably sad.

By the time I'd swept off the patio, the sticks and dead weeds were little more than ash, and the flames in the fire pit had burned themselves out. Brooke had tended that fire with such concentration. "Hey, Brooke," I said, and checked my watch. "Have you eaten lunch yet?"

"No." She shook her head. "Garrett is dropping me back at the house before he has to go to more meetings this afternoon."

"That could work." I took off my garden gloves and tucked them in the back pocket of my jeans.

"What could?"

"Give me just a second," I said, and started for the house. I stopped only long enough on the back porch to peel off my boots before stepping into the kitchen.

Gabriella and Garrett were seated at the table with her laptop, going over a stack of notes.

"Excuse me," I said and waited for Garrett to

focus on me. "How long are your meetings scheduled to run today, Garrett?"

He frowned. "Until this evening."

"You won't be home until after supper?" I wanted to clarify.

"No." He massaged the back of his neck. "I probably won't get back to the village until after 7:00pm."

"Perfect." I nodded and grabbed my jacket and purse from the hooks by the back door. "I've got Brooke until then. You can come by and pick her up on your way home tonight."

"That's not necessary," he began.

"I owe her a pizza." I shrugged my jacket on. "Give me your cell phone and I'll put my number in there for you."

Garrett nodded and pulled the latest model cell phone out of his jacket pocket. With a few taps on his screen he opened it up to contacts. I took the phone from him, typed in my number and name, and hit save. "There you go." I handed it back. "Now, send me a text so I have your number."

"Alright." Garrett tapped a message in his phone, and a second later I felt a buzz in my back pocket where I'd tucked my phone.

I pulled the phone free and added his name to my contacts. "We're all set," I said. "If you need anything or want to check in—call or text me."

"This is very kind of you," he said.

I shrugged. "Seems to me that girl deserves a little kindness." I scooped my sneakers from the floor. "See you later," I said and shut the door behind me. I stopped on the back porch to slip on my shoes, and I bundled Brooke up in the truck before she had time to argue.

The pizza place was loud, slightly dingy and perfect. I ordered a pitcher of Dr. Pepper and a large deep dish pizza with mushrooms on one side and pepperoni on the other. When the food was delivered to the table, Brooke's blue eyes popped.

"I believe the promise was for a pizza 'bigger than your head'." I winked at her.

And for the first time, Brooke actually smiled.

She demolished her half of the pizza and was clearly pleased with herself. After lunch, we headed to the garden center...where I proceeded to buy way too many annuals for planting up the first round of window boxes, hanging baskets and containers in the gardens.

"What do you think of these colors together?" I asked Brooke.

"Well," Brooke considered the orange calibrachoa, yellow snapdragons, and coral geraniums I'd chosen. "I sort of like all the orange colors."

"Let's mix it up." I placed a dark purple verbena in with the grouping of coral flowers. "Better," I decided, and added the purple flowers to the shopping cart.

"You're buying purple, red and orange?" Brooke stood raptly studying all of the flowers in the cart.

"Of course. I like the warm and cool colors all mixed together." I tried to sound casual, "What color flowers do *you* like best, Brooke?"

"Pink, maybe." She jerked a shoulder. "Why?"

"Because you need to pick out some flowers for your own basket."

"You want *me* to plant something?" Brooke blinked.

"Of course." I pointed out some hot pink calibrachoa. "You could make a hanging basket with all pink flowers, it would match your cast."

Brooke's face lit up. "How many of the calibr—" she stumbled over the word.

"Calibrachoa," I said. "Some folks call them 'million bells'."

"How many million bells should I choose?"

"Pick out three containers," I suggested as I felt my phone vibrate. I pulled it from my pocket and checked. Garrett had texted, asking how Brooke was doing.

I sent back a thumbs up emoji and while the girl was engrossed in picking out her own flowers, I snuck a quick picture of her and texted it back to Garrett.

"These remind me of tiny petunias." Brooke held up a pack of hot pink flowers. "Can I put some verbena in my basket too?"

"Sure, the would be pretty trailing over the sides." We shifted to another table and I picked up a cell pack. "What do you think of this white and pink combo of verbena?" I asked.

"I like it."

I watched as she made her selections and added them to the cart. "You've got a good eye."

Once we finished with our selections, we rolled the carts to the checkout. Max had some khaki colored embroidered ball caps for sale, and I purchased one for Brooke.

"Here you go." I tugged the *River Road Garden Center* cap over her bright hair. "This will help protect your nose from the sun."

"That's why you wear a cap when your working in the yard?" she wanted to know.

"Exactly," I said as she checked her reflection in the store windows.

"Dru." Brooke eyeballed the two carts filled with annuals. "Are you really going to plant all of these today?"

"No," I said, putting my wallet back in my purse. "*We* are."

We hauled our loot back to the house, set up in the potting shed, and went to work, while the kittens decided to try and climb up the stacks of mulch and potting soil. The black and gray kitten was content to sleep in the middle of the potting bench, so long as her favorite human was close by. Brooke caught on quickly and, even working one-handed, was enjoying herself.

While she happily planted her own hanging basket, I finally broached the topic of the bullies at her school. I psyched myself up and tried to keep it light. "Well champ, are you ready to face off with your arch nemesis tomorrow?"

Brooke brushed potting soil off her jaw with a shoulder. "I am."

"What was that girl's name?" I acted like I'd forgotten. "Grapefruit or something?"

"Clementine." she giggled. "And she got suspended for a week."

"Reeeeeally?" I drug the word out, and Brooke snickered again.

"She did." Brooke carefully added the trailing pink verbena to her basket. "I guess another girl saw what happened in the bathroom, and she told a teacher. Garrett went to my school last week and he told Mrs. Huntley, our house keeper, that he'd had a *serious conversation* with my principal."

"Oh? Well don't leave me in suspense!" I

encouraged her to keep talking. It was the most words she'd put together all day. "What else did you find out?"

"Well..." Brooke shrugged. "I didn't get to overhear very much."

"Sweetheart," I said, rotating the basket for her, "we really need to work on your spying skills."

"I'll get better at it," she said so earnestly that my stomach dropped.

Ooops, I though. *Note to self: be more careful with what I suggest to an eleven year old.*

Brooke finished up her basket and patted the soil down as I'd shown her. "What do you think?" she asked, holding the hanging basket out by the hook.

"It's gorgeous, but we need some pictures," I said, and pulled my phone out of my back pocket. Brooke smiled slightly for the pictures and then openly laughed when I tried for a selfie of us both with the baskets and boxes we'd planted in the background.

When we were finished, I handed her the phone so she could see the pictures. "I like this one," she said, pointing to the picture of her holding the basket.

"I'll send that one to Garrett," I said.

"Do you think he'd like that?" the girl asked, as if she didn't care.

I made myself speak cheerfully. "I'm sure he would. I'll text it to him right now."

"He doesn't like to be interrupted during meetings."

"Brooke, he won't mind. He texted me earlier today to check on you."

She picked up the striped kitten and cuddled it. "He did?"

"Yes, he did," I answered.

"Maybe you should take a couple more pictures. Of me with Tabby, and send those too."

"Tabby?"

Brooke dropped a kiss between the kitten's ears. "It's what I've been calling her. Besides, a picture would be a good reminder to him that I want a kitten, don't you think?"

"Sweetheart," I sighed, and aimed my phone again. "You're about as subtle as a brick to the forehead."

CHAPTER SEVEN

I kept the girl entertained for the rest of the day, and she blossomed under the attention. We hung up the three hanging baskets on the front porch, and the pair of window boxes were added to the kitchen windows that faced the back. Finally, it was time to wrangle the two large containers that we'd planted. It took both Gabriella and I to lift them. Brooke was game, and she insisted on helping—albeit with her one good arm.

I adjusted the last pot, the largest one that featured mostly red colored flowers, to the edge of the patio that held the Adirondack chairs and the fire pit.

Brooke came out of the potting shed. "Dru, I've got the last six packs of pansies, and the what did you call it?"

"Alyssum," I said. "It symbolizes 'worth beyond beauty'."

Brooke shrugged. "It smells good, anyway."

"Take them all over by the faery statue." I pointed to it. "We'll plant them there."

"You're gonna wear that kid out," Gabriella said to me quietly.

"It's all part of my master plan." I rubbed my hands together, made my sister chuckle, and went over to join Brooke.

One-handed, the girl had started hacking at the soil around the base of the concrete statue. "Like this?" she asked.

I eased the garden trowel away from her. "Let me give you a hand."

"You probably should, since I only have one," Brooke said straight-faced.

I stopped digging. "Did you make a joke?"

Brooke tugged her cap down. "Maybe."

"I'll tell you what," I said. "I'll dig the holes, you plant the flowers around Bluebell."

"You named the statue?" Brooke placed a couple of pansies in the first hole.

I patted the reading faery on the head.

"Please, show some respect. She's a star now, aren't you, Bluebell?" I snipped off a pansy blossom and laid it across her open book.

"A star?" Brooke frowned at me.

"Bluebell was the inspiration for my books," I explained, and continued to dig.

"You write books?" Brooke planted some of the alyssum.

"Children's books," I answered. "About a flower faery named Bluebell and her adventures in an enchanted garden."

Brooke tilted her head. "You really believe in faeries?"

I dug another hole and fat earthworms wriggled up. "Of course I believe in faeries. Don't you?"

Brooke yanked another pansy from its cell pack. "Maybe. I don't know." At her words a few of last year's acorns fell out of the oak tree and plopped on her head. "Hey!" She scowled at the oak tree.

"That's a shame." I considered the big tree. It was almost eighty years old and was undoubtedly wiser than any of us. "Maybe you need to pay attention to what is going on around you in nature." I picked up one of the acorns. "Did you know that the Druids considered the oak to be their most sacred, magickal tree?"

The girl rubbed her head and considered me carefully. "They did?"

I handed the acorn to her. "Wise women believe that carrying an acorn in your pocket helps to ward off illness and remove aches and pains."

"You're saying, I should like...keep this with me?"

"You should." I nodded. "The oak tree gifted it to you, didn't he?"

"He *gifted* it right on top of my head," Brooke grumbled.

"Maybe he was trying to get your attention." I bit my lip and tried to speak calmly. "If I were you, I'd carry that acorn as a good luck charm, it might help your wrist heal faster."

Brooke studied me and slowly slipped the acorn in her pocket. "Most grownups don't believe in faeries or magick."

"Magick is everywhere Brooke, sometimes you simply have to have an open heart to experience it." As I spoke, a robin landed a few feet away from where we were kneeling. Brooke sucked in a breath at the bird being close. I knew what the bird was after, and I picked up a worm and tossed it to him. With a happy tweet it scooped it up from the ground and flew away, right over my head and towards the front of the house.

"You fed that bird." Brooke's voice was awed.

"His mate has a nest in the pussy willow hedges in the front yard. He's taking a snack to her."

"Really?" she asked, considering the hedges. "Can I go see?"

"Sure," I said. "While you do that, I'm going to get the hose and give everything a good drink. After that, we should be done for the day." I stood up and brushed at the potting soil and garden dirt that clung to my clothes.

Brooke got up, but went to sit in one of the Adirondack chairs instead of searching for the bird's nest. She leaned back and rested while I gave all the new containers and flowers a good soaking. "My jeans are dirty." She suddenly sat bolt upright at the discovery. "*I'm* dirty."

"Funny thing about gardening," I said from across the yard. "You work with soil—you get dirty."

"Mrs. Huntley is going to kill me."

I noted she didn't sound particularly concerned...more resigned. "You can always take a shower here, and toss your clothes in the wash before you go home." I purposefully kept my tone light. "It's not a big deal."

"What about my cast in the shower?" Brooke wondered.

"We'll wrap a plastic bag around it." I made a mental note to Google exactly how to protect a cast from water.

"What would I wear while my clothes are being washed?" she asked.

I drug the hose past her. "Cammy probably has a few things you can borrow."

***

By the time Garrett came to pick her up that evening Brooke was sleeping on the couch. Still wearing her cap, and in the sweat pants and t-shirt I commandeered from Camilla's room, she was snoozing under a crocheted afghan that my Gran had made.

Garrett came to a dead stop when he walked into the living room. "She's asleep?"

"I did my best to keep her busy today." I picked up a recycled grocery bag that held her freshly laundered and folded clothes. "Here's her things." I handed them over.

"Her things?" He wrinkled his forehead.

"She got dirty planting flowers, so she took a shower, and we washed her clothes."

"Oh," he said.

Brooke sat upright at our voices. "I'm awake." She pushed the afghan aside and shoved her feet in her shoes.

"Nice hat, Brooke," Garrett said.

"Dru bought it for me." She yawned hugely. "I'm ready to go."

"Thank you for today, Drusilla," Garrett said, while Brooke folded the afghan and set it neatly on the couch.

"It was fun." I nodded. "Good night, Brooke." I said as she shuffled past.

"Thanks Dru," she said.

I picked up her hanging basket from the floor and handed it to Garrett. "This is for your house. Brooke made it."

"She did?" His eyes were round.

"It's great isn't it?" I acted like nothing unusual had happened. "Maybe you could hang it by your front door?"

Garrett recovered quickly. "We certainly can."

Brooke had stopped and waited for his answer about the basket. "Do you like it?" she asked.

"It's beautiful," Garrett said. "We will hang it up as soon as we get back to the house."

"Good luck at school tomorrow," I called as she trooped down the steps. "Don't let that grapefruit get you down."

She gave me a casual wave and, without argument, got in the car.

Garrett hesitated on the porch. "Thank you, Drusilla," he said, searching my face.

My heart thudded in my chest while I gazed into those eerie colored eyes. There was something about the way he studied me, and I had the oddest feeling that if his hands hadn't been full, he would have reached out.

"Goodnight," he finally said.

A breeze came through, and the old wind chimes on the porch rang out. The sound made goose bumps rise on my skin. "Goodnight, Garrett," I said, crossing my arms against the sudden chill.

He went down the steps, carrying the basket of flowers and the bag of clothes. I stayed where I was, watching him. I blew out a slow, careful breath once he climbed in his car, and managed a friendly wave goodbye to the pair of them as he backed out of the driveway and headed home.

The sharp scent of the geraniums I'd planted in the hanging baskets suddenly wafted towards me. "Yes, your message is right on target," I said quietly to the flowers. "I'd have to be pretty dumb to look that way, wouldn't I?"

Out of the corner of my eye I caught motion, and the hanging basket a few feet away began to spin, slowly but surely. I didn't bother searching for the cause of the manifestation. I knew damn good and well the faeries in the yard were trying to communicate.

In the language of flowers, the geranium had several different meanings. However, the most common one was: foolishness.

I considered the pretty coral geraniums in their mixed hanging basket. I reached up for the closest one and a little shower of petals fell into my outstretched hand. "It's alright," I said. "There's absolutely no need to apologize for pointing out my own folly."

The wind chimes rang out again as if in answer, and quietly I let myself back in the house.

***

I spent the next week scraping the peeling paint from around the windows and shutters. I rented a power washer too, and it did wonders to remove the grime from the siding. I turned the spray on the gazebo as well, and just like magick it appeared one hundred percent better.

Once everything was dry, Ella and I began painting all the shutters, trim and doors in a deep midnight blue. Finally, I started work on repairing the crooked shutters on the front of the farmhouse. I did have to dragoon Max to help me with that last chore, but he didn't seem to mind.

I stood in the front yard at sunset with Max, smiling over the fresh paint and rehung shutters. "That's much better," I said. The fact that every muscle in my body was killing me, and I'd broken all my fingernails, didn't bother me in the least. I was beyond happy to see my family home looking the way it should, once again.

"I can't believe how much you've accomplished in the past few weeks." Max slung a friendly arm over my shoulders.

"Thank you for your help," I said to Max. "I couldn't have done all this without you."

"No need to thank me. Around here it's called being neighborly." Max adjusted his ball cap.

"Well, *neighbor*," I smiled up at him. "Let me buy you dinner."

"I think Ella is grilling some chicken for us," Max smiled, affably.

I noted his easy use of the family nickname for my sister, but instead of commenting on it, I tucked my arm in his. "At least let me buy you a beer."

I escorted him in the house, where my sister had a cold beer ready for Max, and a glass of wine waiting for me.

The days were growing warmer as we moved into the month of May, and the snowball bush set its blossoms in pale green spheres. The daffodils finished their show and the tulips took over in bright candy colors. The 'Korean Spice' viburnum shrubs started to show a tiny bit of color and teased the garden with their spicy fragrance. I cleared dead wood out of the Nikko blue hydrangeas and was pleased to see they were also setting huge blossoms. The Shasta daisies, I noted, were growing by leaps and bounds and were probably in need of thinning out if they continued at the rate they were growing.

The 'Moonshine' yarrow, foxgloves, and purple coneflowers' leaves were plumping up nicely and setting buds. The formal herb gardens were still struggling to push out new growth however, so I set aside a nice sunny day to give them a hard pruning.

The alliums were in full bloom, and their purple globes encouraged me to have *patience* while I worked my way around the circular herb bed. I pruned back the varieties of parsley, sage, angelica, and thyme. I made a mental note to purchase new dill and, of course, rosemary plants for the garden. The winters in Illinois were simply too cold for the tender plants to survive our temperatures.

While the birds sang from the safety of the oak tree, Mama cat allowed her brood to romp in the thick spring grass, and I filled up a five-gallon bucket with old dead foliage and stems. Content and happy with the world in general, I glanced over at my phone when it buzzed. Then I did a double take at the text messages I'd received.

Five minutes later I was still sitting on the brick path, staring at two texts. The last thing I'd ever expected to receive was a text message from Garrett Rivers inviting me to his house for dinner.

Brooke and I would like to have you over for dinner tomorrow night. 6:00pm.

Following that text had been: *See? I can*

send a text message. I hear all the cool kids are doing it now.

"He's probably trying to say thank you for helping with Brooke," I told myself. I set my phone down beside me and clipped back the dead wood out of a massive lavender plant. "He didn't ask you on a date...the message said 'Brooke and I'. And I'm not even interested in dating."

I reached out and clipped off more deadwood. "Besides, I'm probably imagining that whole two seconds on the porch," I muttered. "He wouldn't have reached out for me. I'm overreacting..." I managed about a minute and a half before I grabbed my phone to re-read the texts. My lips twitched over the sly humor. "Who knew the man could even make a joke?"

"What man?" Came my grandmother's voice.

I shifted and watched as my Gran made her way steadily down the path with only a cane. As predicted, she'd rid herself of the hated walker. "Hi Gran," I said.

"Good, you're cleaning up the 'Hidcote'.

That lavender plant is getting too woody." She waited a beat. "What man, Drusilla?"

"Hmm?" I tried to act nonchalant.

"Sweetheart, you still talk to yourself when you're stressed, upset, or thinking things over."

With a sigh, I simply handed her the phone. "I'm not sure what to make of this."

Gran read the messages and sent me a withering look. "It's not that difficult, my girl. He invited you to dinner."

"But why?" I adjusted the cap on my head. "What does it mean and what is the correct way to respond?"

"You're too suspicious. What does the garden tell you?" Gran asked.

I snipped off another leggy section of the lavender. "Maybe the lavender is influencing me. It does signify *distrust*."

"The herb is also good for soothing the passions and trembling of the heart," Gran shot back.

"My heart doesn't tremble," I said firmly. *Liar,* my inner voice hissed. *He made your heart pound the other night on the porch...*

Gran let out an aggrieved sigh. "I will never

understand why young people make things so complicated these days."

About a million reasons why it *was* potentially complicated ran through my mind, but I hesitated to tell my grandmother any of them. I stood up, dumped the clippings from the bucket into the wheelbarrow and found my grandmother grinning from ear to ear.

"There you go. I took care of it for you," she said, holding out my phone. "I told him you'd be delighted to come to dinner."

"What exactly did you send?" I scowled at her.

"Oh, don't worry Drusilla, it was a perfectly polite message." She casually brushed at her hair. "I may have mentioned something about you anticipating an evening of unbridled sexual frenzy..."

With a horrified squeak, I grabbed the phone to see exactly what my grandmother had texted back.

The text read: *Thank you. See you at 6:00.*

"That's not funny, Gran!" I said, as she doubled over from laughter.

"Yes, it was." She wiped her eyes. "Pick out

something nice to wear tomorrow, and be sure you give yourself a manicure before you go. Your nails are a mess."

I frowned at my grandmother, who had headed back for the house. She was still chuckling when she let herself inside.

***

I arrived at the old brick home a few minutes before six o'clock. Seeing it up close made the current restoration only more impressive. The original portion of the house had been remodeled in the 1850's into the more elaborate Italianate style. The red brick had been repointed and all of the fancy bracket cornices, the cupola, and Juliette balcony were all freshly painted in gleaming white. I approved of the black shutters on the lower level, and dark, glossy front door. Interestingly, planting beds were roughed in out front, which meant that Garrett had accepted Max's landscaping plans.

I checked my appearance in the rearview mirror. I'd layered a pale pink blazer over a white scoop neck t-shirt, and wore navy, slim fitting slacks. The jacket and slacks were from my Chicago days, but I'd added a few changes, such as my long dangling silver faerie pendant and simple rose quartz earrings. Instead of heels, I'd opted for dark flats. Finally, I'd clipped my hair up in a French twist and left a few tendrils hanging.

I climbed out of my car and decided it was a good compromise, dressing down my fancier pieces with the more casual shirt and bohemian jewelry. I knocked on the front door, checked the rose pink nail polish on my shorter nails, and saw that the hanging basket Brooke had planted was dangling from a wrought iron hook, and growing nicely.

A middle-aged woman answered the door. "Hello," she said.

"Hello, I'm Drusilla Midnight."

"I'm Mrs. Huntley, the housekeeper. We've been expecting you," she said, and held the door open.

I did my best not to gawk at the inside of the home. A dark ornate wooden staircase swept up and out of view, the hardwood floors had been restored and all the wainscoting and trim had to have been original. The elaborate woodwork was, quite simply, show stopping.

"Hi Dru!" Brooke came rushing down the stairs, hit the hardwood and slid over to me on her thick socks.

I automatically grabbed her by the arm as she started to skid past me. "Whoa, let's not break your other arm."

Mrs. Huntley rolled her eyes to the ceiling. "Please be more careful, young lady."

Brooke pulled herself up straight. "Yeah, yeah," she said with a long suffering sigh. But I thought I detected a hint of humor in her tone.

"I'm headed home for the evening." Mrs. Huntley pulled her keys from her pocket. "Try and stay out of trouble for a few hours," she said to Brooke.

Brooke shrugged.

"If you can manage to behave yourself and not break any more bones," Mrs. Huntley said, "I'll make snickerdoodles tomorrow."

"Really?" Brooke asked with a gleam in her eye.

Mrs. Huntley reached for the door. "Yes, really. However, I'd better get a glowing report of your good behavior."

I raised my hand. "I can promise I'll be on my best behavior. I *love* snickerdoodles."

"Ha, ha. Very funny," Brooke said.

"I'm dead serious. That's my favorite cookie," I said, making Mrs. Huntley chuckle.

"It was nice to meet you," the woman said, and let herself out the door.

"You too." I said.

The housekeeper was shaking her head as she left, but she was smiling.

"How is your arm doing?" I asked Brooke as soon as we were alone. "Are you still keeping that acorn with you?"

"I am." She pulled it from the pocket of her shorts. "I guess it can't hurt."

"I saw your hanging basket out front." I smiled. "It looks very happy there."

"*Looks* happy?" Brooke tilted her head to one side. "You're weird, Dru."

"I'll take that as a compliment," I said. "Where's your uncle?"

"He's not my uncle—" Brooke began.

"Fine," I cut her off. "Where's Garrett?"

"In the kitchen." Brooke grabbed my hand

and tugged. "It's back this way."

"He cooks?" I couldn't help but ask.

"Not very well," Brooke confided. "Mrs. Huntley made dinner for us, he only has to serve it."

Not sure what to expect, I followed the girl through the house and toward a big, bright, white kitchen. I summed up the room in seconds. Dark hardwood floors ran throughout the space, the cabinets were high and obviously new, the long countertops appeared to be a pale gray granite.

Garrett, I discovered, was standing by the stove, carving a pretty roast chicken that rested on a platter. Bowls of mashed potatoes, dinner rolls, and cooked carrots were already waiting on an old farmhouse style table under the windows.

"She's here!" Brooke announced.

Garrett lifted the platter, yet his eyes zeroed in on me instantly. "Hello, Drusilla."

"Hello," I nodded politely. "Dinner smells wonderful."

"Mrs. Huntley's roast chicken," he said.

I'd never seen him dressed so casually. He

wore a pale blue, button down shirt with the sleeves rolled up to his elbows, dark jeans, and scuffed trainers. I yanked my eyes away from his clothes and fell back on the manners that Gran had drilled in my head. "Can I help with anything?"

"Not a thing," he assured me. His eyes met mine and he smiled. Slowly.

Suddenly nervous, my heart slammed against my ribs. *I had absolutely no reason to feel nervous*, I told myself. *Because this wasn't a date.* Still, I stood there trapped in those mystical blue-green eyes for a few seconds. I blinked, and shook myself out of his influence.

"Come on, I'm starving." Brooke pulled me to the table.

Somehow, Garrett beat us there and he gallantly pulled out a chair for me. "Thank you," I said, and sat in the chair between the two of them.

Brooke plopped down and reached immediately for a roll.

"Brooke." Garrett's voice was quiet but firm as he placed the chicken on the table. "Wait until after everyone has been served."

Brooke grumbled and placed the roll on her plate. Garrett served slices of chicken, and Brooke began to pass the food. For a few moments we ate in companionable silence.

Garrett poured a glass of white wine for me. I murmured my thanks, sipped, and realized it was the same wine Gabriella had served my first night home. "What wine is this?"

"It's from a local winery," Garrett said.

"It's *our* winery," Brooke said impatiently.

"Your winery?" I reached for the bottle. "*Trois Amis*," I read the label.

"It means: three friends," Brooke said around a mouthful of mashed potatoes.

"We're having the grand opening this summer," Garrett said.

Suddenly it clicked. Gabriella had said the wine she'd served was from a new local winery. She'd been working with him a lot lately on his website, as the launch date was getting closer.

"You own a winery?" I asked.

"I own a third of it. Originally there were three of us," Garrett said.

"*Trois Amis*," I said.

"My best friends Philippe Marquette and

Barry James, we all started the business together five years ago."

"Marquette," I said, recognizing the name. "The Marquettes are one of the founding families of Ames Crossing. If I remember correctly they used to have vineyards in the early 1900's but the family had a run of bad luck."

"That's right," Garrett said.

"And your other partner, Barry James?" I asked.

"That was my dad," Brooke said. "Now I'm the third person in the *trois amis*."

CHAPTER EIGHT

Over dinner, Garrett told me how his first cousin Melissa Rivers and his friend Barry James had met, fallen in love and gotten married after college. The three friends, Philippe, Barry and Garrett, had decided to work together and invest in the old Marquette family vineyards and to open a winery.

Philippe had been working with the vintner and the vineyard team for the past few years. He'd also begun the extensive work required for the restoration of his ancestral home. Garrett had purchased the Italianate house in the village with plans of turning it into a winery themed B&B. Meanwhile, Barry had dealt with the legal end of things with the plan to relocate his family to Ames Crossing six months before the grand opening. But tragedy had struck, and he and his wife had died, and Garrett was named as a guardian to his cousin's child.

"The third part of the winery is being held in a trust for Brooke until she becomes twenty-one." Garrett explained.

"Wow," I studied the girl. "I'm sitting at the table with an eleven-year-old business woman."

"I guess." A small smile appeared on Brooke's face. "Philippe and Garrett, they let me help with some things."

"Such as?" I asked.

"I picked out the design for the labels. Garrett and Philippe kept arguing about it, so I got to break the tie."

I studied the bottle and its stylized *fleur de lis* design. "Did you know that the *fleur de lis* is thought to be an iris flower?"

"No, I didn't," Garrett said.

I shifted my eyes to him. "That's the reason you've been busy, and having all of those meetings lately."

"We are less than a month away from the Grand Opening," Garrett said. "It's been a little hectic."

"There's going to be a big fancy party when it all opens," Brooke announced. "Up at Philippe's haunted house on the cliffs."

"The Marquette house isn't haunted, Brooke," Garrett said.

"It *looks* haunted," she argued back.

"Wait, are you talking about the old Marquette Mansion on Notch Cliff?" I asked.

"Yes." Garrett nodded.

"I'm going to have to side with Brooke on this one," I said. "That place *is* creepy and with all the crumbling stonework it's like something out of a gothic horror movie."

"See." Brooke crossed her arms. "I told you."

"When I was in school, we used to dare each other to go up there." I nudged Brooke with my elbow. "Under a full moon of course."

"Did you ever see any ghosts?" she wanted to know.

"I didn't." I picked up my wine. "But Camilla swears to this day that she saw a woman in white on the third floor."

"A woman in white?" Garrett gave me an incredulous look.

"Really?" Brooke leaned forward.

"Ask her about it sometime," I encouraged the girl.

"Now you've done it," Garrett groaned and rolled his eyes. "Brooke is fascinated by the paranormal."

"Oh, do you want to be a paranormal investigator someday?" I asked her.

"Maybe," she said. "I thought for a while this house was haunted...but Garrett said it was just old plumbing."

She sounded so disappointed that I fought to keep a serious expression. "And are you still planning to make this house into a B and B?"

"No," Garrett poured himself a second glass of wine. "When Brooke came to live with me, I decided to have this become our home instead. I liked the charm of the village, the people and the small businesses."

Garrett said that lightly, but I realized that he'd completely altered his life for the girl, and that impressed me.

"We made some changes to the original plans, with the focus on this being a home, not an inn." He smiled. "Living here during the renovations was wild, wasn't it Brooke?"

"It took forever," she said. "The widow's walk and cupola still aren't finished."

"It can wait." Garrett ate the last of his chicken.

"It's a beautiful home," I said to Garrett. "And I agree with you about living in Ames Crossing. It's a wonderful place for a child to grow up."

"I hate going to Saint Mary's," Brooke said of her school.

"After everything you've been through, I don't blame you." Meal over, I stood and started stacking plates.

Her bottom lip poked out. "I want to go to a public school instead. They don't wear uniforms."

I checked Garret's expression. This was obviously an old argument, and the last thing I wanted to do was cause any further discord. I carried the plates to the sink. "That's something you and Garrett should discuss together, as a family."

"I hate school." Brooke pouted.

"Well, that's too bad," I said easily. "It takes a lot of study to become a parapsychologist.

Even a good ghost hunter needs to know their history."

Brooke scowled at me. "They do?"

"Camilla and her college friends are a part of a group that does paranormal investigations," I explained to Brooke. "And in case you wondered, Camilla's getting degrees in historic preservation *and* history."

"History is boring." Brooke made a face. "Do I still have to clean up the kitchen tonight, Garrett?"

"Yes you do," he cut her off in mid-whine. "Your punishment for ditching school was KP for a month."

Brooke sighed loudly. "Fine."

In a few short minutes Garrett transferred the leftovers into storage containers and slipped them in the fridge. Basically all the girl had to do was load the dishwasher and wipe down the table and counters. Garrett escorted me to their family room, and it was a pretty space, with the old dark wood wainscoting and trim, but with modern paint colors and more comfortable up-to-date furniture.

I took my wineglass to the fireplace and

studied the elaborately carved heraldry that hung above the mantle. "It's a twin tailed mermaid," I said.

"This carving belonged to my grandfather," Garrett said, joining me. "It's a romantic version of the Rivers' family crest.

Well that fits, I thought fatalistically. *The first time I saw him at the river I'd wondered if he was a Siren or water spirit.* Gazing up at Melusine, I tipped my head in respect. There were plenty of families from France who claimed to be descendants from the river goddess. I snuck a quick glance at him. *It might explain the eyes...* I shook myself out of my thoughts and decided it best not to bring up the topic of goddesses. After all, I had no idea how he would react to it. "It's a lovely old carving," I said instead, and sipped my wine.

"Listen, while we have a moment alone," Garrett said, "I want to thank you. I'm not sure what you did, but you've made more progress with Brooke than we've been able to accomplish in over a year."

"I only spent some time with her in the gardens." I recalled what Max had said to me when I'd thanked him for his help. "It's called being neighborly."

Garrett reached out and touched my arm. "It's more than that," he said, angling his body towards mine.

Flustered, I looked up, and was trapped in his eyes. The colors shifted from blue, to green, and finally to aqua. "I'm glad I was able to help," I managed.

"Drusilla." His voice was low, and he began to slowly move in. I felt his fingertips gently brush down and rest at the inside of my wrist.

"What are you doing?" I heard myself whisper.

Garrett paused and searched my face. His mouth inches from mine, he continued to gaze into my eyes, and wait silently. I counted my heartbeats. *One, two, three.* However, he didn't press forward.

I held perfectly still.

So did he.

Neither of us moved, but instead, measured the other.

He continued to hold his ground, and even as my heart trembled I ultimately was the one who eased back. When I did, I found that my palms were sweaty. In desperation, I set my wineglass down on the mantle before I dropped it.

Intending to be firm, I shifted back to face him. "Garrett," I began, squaring my shoulders. "I'm not interested in casual dating at this time."

His lips twitched slightly. "Neither am I."

Caught off guard, I frowned over his words. "Well, if you think that because I'm newly divorced I'd be happy to hop into bed with the first man who shows a little interest, allow me to disabuse you of that notion."

His expression was grave, even as he inclined his head. "That's good to know."

I scowled at him. "Are you making fun of me?"

"No, I'm not," he said, and his eyes took on a strange light that had my mouth going dry. "But I'm fascinated with you, Drusilla, and I'd like to get to know you better."

I frowned, not quite sure what to make of him. "We'll just see about that."

One side of his mouth kicked up. "We certainly will."

Anything else that would have been said, or done, ended because Brooke came into the room, blissfully unaware of the tension.

***

The next morning, I hadn't slept well and felt out of sorts, as I'd spent most of the night repeatedly going over in my mind what had happened at Garrett's house.

I put on a basic face: sunscreen, foundation, mascara and black eyeliner. I brushed my hair into a ponytail and resisted the urge to stomp down to breakfast—barely—because it seemed like something Brooke would have done. Instead, I listened with half an ear to my grandmother and sister talk excitedly about the grand opening of the *Trois Amis* Winery in June. Apparently, they were hosting an elaborate masquerade party at that old house up on the cliffs.

Hearing them bubble over about *Garrett this* and *Garrett that* hadn't improved my mood whatsoever.

I'd ducked out when they started discussing

what they would wear to the party. I made good my escape and was sulking in the potting shed with a big mug of tea while gathering my tools for the day's work in the gardens. But I couldn't concentrate, all I kept seeing in my mind was Garrett's blue-green eyes. I'd never seen eyes that color. Were they turquoise blue, or maybe more of an aquamarine hue?

"And why on earth should it matter anyway?" In frustration, I lightly kicked a bag of mulch. "What's wrong with me? I'm not some quivering virgin to go all misty-eyed over a man moving in for a kiss." I spun back to the bench and came up short when I saw a lone stem of daylily on the old wooden work surface.

I approached it cautiously. Daylilies were not in season yet. The pink blossom was open, and I warily studied the six petals. In wise woman lore the daylily's message was: flirtation.

I slowly scanned my surroundings. There was no movement, and everything was quiet. I sipped my tea and waited, wondering what would manifest next. I saw a flash of color and spotted a male cardinal perched on the top of the open shed door. He chirped a few times, bobbed his head twice, and then flew away.

"I don't think so," I said to whatever nature spirit was listening. According to the old traditions, when a redbird crossed your path, a girl could expect to be kissed before sunset. "I'm hardly a girl anymore," I snorted, "and no one is going to show up to kiss me."

Well...someone almost did last night, a nagging inner voice reminded me.

"Damn it. Now I've graduated from talking to myself—to actively arguing with myself." I set the mug down with a snap, leaned against the workbench, and silently faced the truth.

That almost-kiss was absolutely the sexiest thing that had ever happened to me.

Mama cat made the leap to the potting bench and began to head butt me, wanting some attention. I scooped her up in my arms. "Good morning, Mama cat. Can we talk?" The cat tucked her head over my shoulder, and I took that for an assent. "I suppose I am attracted to him. A little." I patted her back. "Although I shouldn't be."

The Tortoiseshell cat purred loudly in reply.

"He's not even my type." I walked back and forth with the cat contentedly in my arms. "I'm only human, aren't I? And it's been over six months since I've been with anyone."

The cat made a sound somewhere between a chuckle and a chirp.

"Tragic, eh?" I confessed to my feline therapist. "I suppose an honest hormonal reaction to a gorgeous man with spooky eyes is nothing to be embarrassed about, right?"

The cat nuzzled my ear in sympathy and snuggled closer.

"But damn the man anyway, for getting me all stirred up."

The cat began to squirm, and I opened my arms. She hopped to the workbench, sat, and tucked her tail around herself.

I patted her head. "Thanks for the chat," I said.

"Meow," was Mama cat's response.

I picked up the pink lily and twirled the flower. "Now, If I could stop obsessing over the whole incident."

Mama cat lifted a paw and patted my arm, which made me chuckle. I straightened and decided to get to work. "Let's see..." I tucked the flower behind my ear and tried to remember what I'd come out to the shed for in the first place. My mind was completely blank though, and I glanced around at the tools hoping it would jog my memory.

"Hedge trimmers!" I suddenly remembered and slapped a hand to my forehead. "For the boxwood hedges. Come on Dru, pull it together," I muttered, and picked up the big eclectic trimmers; and suddenly spotted Garrett Rivers leaning in the open doorway.

I jolted and bobbled the trimmer. "What are you doing here?"

"What is that?" he asked. "It looks like a weird sort of chain saw."

"It's a hedge trimmer," I said crossly. "For the boxwoods out front."

"If I promise to be a gentleman, you won't turn that on me, will you?"

I rolled my eyes at him and deliberately set the trimmer down on the far end of the work bench. "Why are you here, Garrett?" I asked again.

"I wanted to see you."

I crossed my arms over my chest. "Why?"

"A couple of reasons," he said. "Mrs. Huntley told me she'd like to have some fresh herbs for cooking, and I thought you would have some suggestions on what I should purchase."

The kittens heard the unfamiliar voice and came pouncing across the brick floor straight for Garrett. "Brace yourself," I warned him, and wondered how he'd react to the cat hair that was about to transfer all over his expensive navy blue suit.

"Oh well damn it," he said mildly. He hunkered down and started to pet the kittens. "You guys *are* cute."

My mouth hit the floor as he chuckled over the tiny fur balls, and I caught myself practically sighing over him while he acquainted himself with the five kittens. I straightened my shoulders. *Focus, Drusilla,* I reminded myself sternly. "Brooke favors the—"

"Tabby kitten." He nodded. "I know."

"They should be ready for adopting next week," I said.

He picked up the striped kitten and went

nose to nose. "You're the one, eh?"

The kitten meowed and swatted at Garrett's face. Garrett held the kitten close and it cuddled under his chin. He flashed a smile and my heart skipped a beat.

I made sure that my voice would be steady when I spoke. "I'm going to go out on a limb and guess that the kitten is the other reason you dropped by?"

"It's one of them." he rubbed the kitten's ears and set it down. "We'll take this one, but I'd like to keep it a surprise."

"Brooke is going to be over the moon," I said, and turned my back to gather up the extension cord for the trimmer. I reached over my head and before I knew it, Garrett was behind me, taking it from my hands.

"Allow me." He set the bulky orange cord on the bench.

"Thank you," I said, intending to go about my business, and found that I had no where to go. Garrett was standing right in front of me.

"There's another reason I stopped by." His voice was husky and low.

Silently I searched his eyes, but refused to

play coy and ask what the other reason was.

We both knew what it was.

Garrett wasn't invading my personal space. He was allowing plenty of room for me to duck past him if I'd wished, but for some reason I didn't want to.

He was waiting. For me to accept or to refuse. The fact that he didn't push softened me like nothing else could have.

Entranced, I stared up into his paranormally blue-green eyes. I leaned forward.

Garrett eased farther in as well, but stopped a few inches shy of my mouth.

"What are you waiting for?" I asked.

"You," he said, dropping his mouth down on mine.

A moan escaped that I dimly recognized as coming from me. But I didn't care. Garrett pulled me closer, dipping me back the tiniest bit, and proceeded to kiss whatever sensible reasons I had for not getting involved with anyone ever again—right out of my head.

The kiss went on and on, and when I wrapped my arms around his neck, he picked me up by the hips. I ended up sitting on the sturdy work bench, with Garrett standing between my thighs. His hands reached up and pulled the elastic band from my ponytail, and my hair spilled out and over my shoulders. He sunk his fingers in, cupped the back of my head and pulled me even closer to him.

In response, I hooked my ankles behind his waist, rocked against him, and our kiss went wild.

A loud crash had us pulling apart. I checked for the source of the noise and discovered that a few terra cotta pots had been knocked off the workbench. They were broken and lying on the bricks at his feet. I sat there, still within his arms as we panted together, both trying to catch our breath.

"I'm sorry," I blurted out, dropping my feet and easing back from him slightly.

"I'm not," he said.

"No, I'm sorry for sending mixed signals," I tried to clarify. "The truth is, I'm not quite ready for all of this."

He stepped away slowly, his eyes locked on mine. "When you are ready, Drusilla, you know where to find me."

I shuddered. I couldn't help it, and I fully expected him to have some sort of smug, male comeback to my reaction, but he surprised me.

"Don't overdo it working in the gardens today," he said, gently running a finger across my bottom lip.

That easy touch had my stomach tying itself into knots. "I won't overdo it."

He hesitated at the doorway. "Let me know when it's a good time to pick up the kitten for Brooke."

I found I had to swallow before I could speak. "I will."

"It's costing me to walk away from you right now," he said. "Do you understand?"

"I do understand," I said. "Because honestly, it's costing me to let you."

His eyes flashed. For a moment I thought he might scoop me right up again, but instead he nodded once, and left.

It took everything I had to stay where I was and not do something irresponsible...like run after him. Instead, I waited until I was sure he'd gone, then I eased down from the bench and went to sit in one of the chairs on the back patio and get some air.

I sat down by the big container of flowers. "What just happened in there?" I pushed my hair back and found that my hands were still shaking. As I waited for my system to settle, a male cardinal landed on the arm of the Adirondack chair next to mine. He flapped his wings and began to sing sweetly.

I chuckled. "Yes, you certainly did warn me about the kiss."

I felt a light brush against my hand. The trailing verbena I'd planted with Brooke was now covered in lush, bright red blooms and spilling over the edges of the pot. "Enthralled." I raised my brows at the very accurate meaning of the flower.

Garrett Rivers was a powerful man on many levels; personally, physically, energetically, and possibly...magickally. The fact that his family heraldry featured Melusine might explain why he affected me so. According to legend Melusine was thought to either be a water spirit, a goddess of the river, or a Siren.

But no matter what the underlying cause, I wondered how long it had been since a man had managed to cast a spell of any sort over a daughter of Midnight.

Could I break his enchantment?

Absolutely. I was, after all, surrounded with a garden full of magickal supplies...

However, I wasn't sure that I wanted to.

CHAPTER NINE

The day had finally arrived for the kittens to have new homes. All five of the kittens had been adopted, and Mama cat had an appointment at the vet next week. It was the responsible thing to do, but part of me was sad at the thought of not having any more kittens around the gardens.

I hadn't been sleeping well for the past few days, and when I did manage to sleep my subconscious was filled with sensual images of me with Garrett in the potting shed. In the dreams we hadn't stopped at kissing, and while I considered myself a normal woman with a healthy sex drive...my dreams of late had been downright erotic.

I blamed it on my reading those romance

novels of Gabriella's.

"Alright, Drusilla." I tugged a robin's egg blue t-shirt over my head and proceeded to give myself a firm talking to. "You can handle yourself around Garrett Rivers. You'll go drop off the kitten, keep your hormones firmly under control, make some polite small talk, give the books to Brooke, and afterwards head to the garden center for snapdragons. Easy peasy."

"You still mutter when something's bothering you," my sister said, leaning against my bedroom door.

Caught, I couldn't think of one clever thing to say in reply. Instead, I tugged the hem down over the waist of my jeans and sat on the bed to put my shoes on.

"Did something happen between you and Garrett?" Gabriella brushed her pale blonde hair back from her face.

I slipped on my low-heeled ankle boots. "When did you and Garrett first meet?" I asked her instead.

"About a year and a half ago." She tilted her head. "I met him right after he brought Brooke into town."

"Do you know if he's been seeing anyone socially?" I attempted to make my question sound casual.

My sister's eyes went sharp. "Not that I've been aware of. Why?"

"I was simply curious."

"He's attracted to you." She smiled. "As you are to him."

"My divorce hasn't even been final for two full months," I reminded her, and maybe myself.

Gabriella walked over and sat beside me. "You were separated for six months before the divorce became official." She waited a beat. "What's your next excuse?"

"It's not an excuse," I argued. "I'm hardly in a position to..." I trailed off, and blew out a long breath. "I wasn't expecting any of this," I admitted. "I wasn't looking for him."

She patted my leg. "Are you falling for him?"

"I'm not ready to fall for anyone." I winced, realizing I'd said almost the same to Garrett the week before.

"It's not about being *ready*." Gabriella said

gently.

I tossed my hands up in frustration "Then what *is* it about?"

"Sometimes, someone comes unexpectedly into your life, takes you by surprise, and changes your heart forever." Her voice carried the ring of truth.

I shook my head, not caring for the way the conversation was going. "I hardly think that the sentiment—romantic though it may be—applies to my situation, Ella."

"Is that so?" She tapped a finger to her lips as if thinking it over. "Funny, I saw him go into the potting shed to talk to you the other day; and when you walked out a little while later, your hair was mussed, and you were staggering."

"I was *not* staggering," I insisted.

"Yes, you were." Gabriella grinned. "So, is he a good kisser?"

"Well, I—"

"I figured it was only kissing," she interrupted. "He wasn't in there long enough to do anything else."

"Ella!" I said, mortified.

My sister snorted with laughter. "Oh honey, relax. I'm just saying, Garrett doesn't strike me as a wham-bam-thank-you-ma'am, kind of guy."

"Sounds like you've given this some thought," I said dryly.

"Yeah," she hummed. "It's those sexy sea-blue eyes. He's intense, and I'll bet you that when Garrett Rivers makes love to a woman...she feels lucky to survive it, and wonders how soon until they can do it all over again."

"I think those romance covers have gone to your head."

She gave me a hip bump. "Be honest. Part of you wonders what it'd be like to let loose, and go crazy with him."

"No," I lied. "Absolutely not."

"Aww...that's too bad." Gabriella wiggled her brows. "Well, cheer up. I say you two will christen the shed before the end of the summer."

I dropped my face in my hands. "You're killing me, Ella."

She patted my head. "Come on, let me help

you with your hair before you go and see him."

"I'm dropping off my books, and the kitten for Brooke. I'm *not* going to see him." I glared at her. "And for the record. There's nothing wrong with my hair."

My sister stood and hauled me over to the mirror. "I call bullshit." Before I could comment, she'd tugged the band free from my ponytail. "You've been dressing down, and basically hiding yourself since you came home.

"No, I haven't." I was appalled at the thought. *I hadn't done that...Had I?*

"Yes you have," Gabriella said as if she'd heard my thoughts. "You've been wearing a basic face too, and have had your hair in a severe ponytail for weeks."

"So what?" I asked, defensively. "I've been working in the gardens. Not going to the country club."

She took my comb from the dresser and began working it through my long tresses. "You've got great hair. I'd kill to have straight hair like yours."

"I always wanted wavy hair like yours," I argued.

Gabriella chuckled and nudged my makeup bag closer towards me. "While the master is at work, put on a bit more war paint."

I rolled my eyes at her in the mirror. "Fine, fine." I reached for my eye shadow palette and selected a brush. "What are you doing back there?"

"I'm working your hair into a reversed fishtail braid. I'll muss it up a bit so it's softer." Deftly, Gabriella began the braiding. "But it will still be out of the way and practical. Trust me."

I watched as she braided my dark blonde hair over my shoulder. It wasn't long before she secured the braid with a tie, and then began pulling small sections slightly loose. She brushed my bangs over and sprayed it all with hairspray. "That's very pretty," I said admiring her work. "Thank you."

She picked up my black eyeliner. "Close your eyes," she ordered.

I did, but smirked at her. "When did you get so bossy?"

"Shut up and trust me, Sis."

Finally she finished, and I opened my eyes

slowly, wondering what I'd find in the mirror.

My breath huffed out. The cosmetics were subtle but effective. Gabriella had deepened my taupe and brown eye shadows and managed to make my blue eyes almost mirror the color of my shirt. She'd done some sort of witchery, and my cheekbones appeared more pronounced too.

While I'd been studying the difference, my sister had been rooting around in my closet. She brought over a loosely knit, mauve colored duster length sweater. "Here, let's dress up that t-shirt and jeans a bit."

"It may shock you to know that I can pick out my own clothes," I said, slipping it on. "I've been doing it for years."

"Push up the sleeves. It makes it more casual," she ordered, and began to root through my jewelry box. She selected an oversized pendant of rhodocrosite and looped the long chain over my head.

"There." She nodded her head, satisfied with the results. "You look great. Now go get your man."

"He's not my man. I'm not going over there to *go get* him."

One side of her mouth kicked up. "Well then, make him suffer a bit, and think about you."

I selected a mauve lipstick and slid it over my lips. "I don't want to make him suffer."

"That lipstick will drive him crazy," she pointed out.

"I'm putting it on for me," I said, closing the tube. "Not for him."

"Okay," she said way too cheerfully. "It sure can't hurt." My sister grabbed me by the elbow.

"Wait a second," I said, scooping up my books, and Ella promptly steered me out of the house.

Once the cat carrier was loaded, Gabriella gave me a hug. "Now go make him sweat a little," she said. "Reclaim your power, and reclaim your self."

I thought about her words as I made the short drive to Garrett's house. I pulled in the driveway and glanced at my watch. I was right on time. Telling myself there was no need to double check my appearance, I did so anyway. More nervous than I cared to admit, I drew in a deep breath, tucked the books under my arm, and took the carrier around the side of the house to the kitchen door.

Mrs. Huntley was waiting for me. "Come in, quick!" She tugged me inside.

"Hello," I whispered, setting the carrier on the big kitchen table.

Mrs. Huntley bent over to see the meowing kitten. "Oh, she's adorable." The house keeper was all smiles as she tugged me to stand next to her. "Here they come."

I could hear Brooke and Garrett coming down the hall, and I wiped the grin off my face and stayed glued to the housekeeper's side so Brooke wouldn't see the carrier when she walked in.

"We need to have a talk about responsibility..." Garrett's voice preceded them into the kitchen. He was dressed casually again in jeans, and a pale gray Henley style shirt.

"I cleaned up the kitchen every night for a month," Brooke grumbled as they walked in.

"Yes you did. But now you're going to have to be responsible for more than just yourself," Garrett said.

"Huh?" Brooke's face scrunched up in confusion when she spotted me leaning against the table. "Hi Dru. I didn't know you were coming over."

"I brought you my books. I thought you might want to read them."

"Oh, cool," Brooke said. "I'll check them out."

"That was very thoughtful." Garrett nudged Brooke. "Maybe you should say thank you to Drusilla."

"Thanks Dru." Brooke frowned at me as I continued to lean against the table. "Is something going on?"

"I had another reason for dropping by," I said as the kitten let out a high-pitched meow from the carrier. At the sound, Brooke's eyes went huge in her face. Garrett gave me a nod, and I stepped aside allowing the girl to see the carrier.

"There's a kitten needing a home of her own," Garrett said. "I thought maybe you'd like to help out with that."

Brooke's jaw dropped. "*What*?"

"Surprise." Garrett rested his hand on her shoulder. "What do you think, Brooke?"

Brooke stared up at him. "Really? I can keep

her?" She pressed her hands over her mouth and promptly burst into tears.

Garrett seemed horrified at Brooke's noisy reaction. I scooped the kitten out of the carrier and brought it over to the girl. "She's yours now," I said gently over her tears.

Brooke took the kitten and held her close, sobbing over the kitten. "She's mine? *Really*?"

"She certainly is," I patted her shoulder.

"I bought some kitten food," Garrett began, sounding unsure.

"There's new food bowls and a litter box as well," Mrs. Huntley said while Brooke wiped her eyes. "Be sure you show her where the box is, right away."

Brooke threw one arm around Garrett and hugged him. "Thank you!"

He held on for a moment and ran his hand down the girl's bright hair. "You're welcome." He grinned down at the kitten between them. "I suppose we better think of a name."

"I want to call her Tabby," Brooke said.

"That's a good name." I couldn't help but smile at the two of them.

For the next half hour Brooke was in kitten

heaven showing off her new pet to Mrs. Huntley, and when Garrett produced a hot pink kitten collar Mrs. Huntley helped her put it on the cat. Tabby wasn't sure what to make of the collar at first, but after a few moments of scratching at it she began to romp around the kitchen floor to the music of the bell on her collar.

Garrett's mystical colored eyes locked on mine. "Can I speak to you in private?" he asked.

"I have to run to the nursery and pick up some snapdragons," I said, and internally cheered at how casual I'd made that statement sound.

"Snapdragons?" He smiled down in my face. "Sounds serious."

My stomach quivered, even as I pulled off what I hoped was a serene nod. "Yes, snapdragons. For the gardens at the front of the farmhouse."

"Mrs. Huntley," Garrett said, his eyes never leaving my face. "Drusilla and I will be right back." Without further ado he politely took me by the arm and escorted me out of the kitchen and into another room.

I walked along with him, outwardly calm while my mind raced. *Damn the man for making me nervous!* A bead of sweat ran between my shoulders. *Wasn't I supposed to be making him sweat?* I thought, straightening my spine.

"What do you use this room for?" I asked, taking in the dark wood book shelves. "It's lovely." There. My voice sounded perfectly composed and I had my hormones on a tight rein. Hooray for control.

He smoothly slid a pocket door shut behind us. "I'm using it for a home office at the moment."

"Oh." Belatedly, I spotted his desk and computer. "This is nice." Determined to *not* let him know how nervous he made me, I shifted back to face him. "I especially like the green paint you—"

My words were cut off by a firm kiss. I'd been so busy trying to project polished sophistication, that I never even saw him coming. It was a soft closed mouth kiss to start, then he ran his tongue across the seam in my lips, encouraging me to open to him, and I shuddered.

His hands were framed on either side of my face, and delicately he began to brush the lightest of kisses along the sides of my mouth.

I suppose all the frustration of a week's worth of erotic dreams got the better of me, and I refused to simply stand there submissively. With that thought in mind, I wrapped my arms around his waist, pulled him closer and swept my tongue inside of *his* mouth. Maybe I was, as Ella had said, reclaiming my power. Either way, it was a huge rush.

Garrett jolted in response, and I pressed even closer. While our tongues dueled, one of his hands fastened on the braid of my hair while the other skimmed lightly down my breast. Now it was my turn to jump in reaction to his explorations.

The sound of Brooke's laughter right outside the door had us breaking apart.

I stared up into those jewel-bright eyes and felt my heart do a flip with a double twist, and then...it fell. *Oh no,* I thought as it landed with a hard splat. *The landing was a little rough. Dru may have to settle for the bronze.*

My inner monologue was so randomly ridiculous that I fought against the giggles. I bit my lip to keep the nervous laughter from escaping as the metallic sound of jingle bells were followed by Brooke's footsteps as she pursued the kitten down the hall.

"I shouldn't have started this," he whispered, and we both held our breaths as Brooke chased the kitten past the closed door again.

"You have my lipstick on your mouth." I tried to wipe it off with my thumb.

He ran his tongue across his own lips and tasted the lipstick. He closed his eyes on a hum of pleasure. "I promised myself I wouldn't touch you again until we were truly alone."

I gulped. That sound he'd made and the words he'd spoken went straight to my belly. Testing, I ran my thumb over *his* bottom lip again, and was delighted by the light that came into his eyes. I started to lean forward...

"Hey guys!" Brooke was at the door.

I dropped my hand, and we stepped apart with simultaneous groans.

She slid the door open with a bang. "You've

gotta see what Tabby is doing!"

"Be right there," Garrett assured her.

I used that as an opportunity to try and make an exit. "I should go, and see about getting those flowers for the gardens."

"The snapdragons aren't going anywhere." Garrett caught my hand. His voice was husky and low. "Stay for dinner."

"Tonight?"

"I'll call Max and ask him to put some flowers aside. He'll hold them for you."

"Oh." I hadn't expected him to think of that. "I wanted pink ones."

"It can be arranged." He smiled. "Please stay. I'd like to spend some time with you."

I felt my lips curve. "It happens that my calendar is open this evening."

To my surprise, I found myself relaxing and enjoying his company. He gave me a tour of the house, while Brooke kept watch over her new kitten. I thought we'd go out for dinner, but Garrett ended up grilling a few steaks on a gas grill on the new paver patio behind the house. I put a salad together with the supplies he had in the kitchen, and Brooke sat on the patio, reading out loud from my books to her kitten who had fallen asleep in her lap.

Since the weather was nice we decided to sit around the patio table and eat our dinner alfresco. Brooke held the snoozing kitten in her lap as we ate, and she was the most animated I'd ever seen her.

"I like your books, Dru," Brooke announced.

I swallowed a bite of salad. "Thank you."

"I thought they'd be for little kids, but Bluebell, she's kinda cool."

"I had a hunch you'd enjoy reading about her adventures."

"The pictures inside are awesome. Did you draw them?"

"No, I have an artist that I work with." When Brooke wanted to know how that worked, I explained. "The artist reads the story, and we talk about what I think would work the best. She works up preliminary sketches and once I approve them, she watercolors—paints the drawings."

"Oh, I get it." Brooke nodded.

In my opinion, everything was going wonderfully, until Brooke surprised me with an uncomfortable change in topics.

"Dru, how come you don't have any kids?" she asked. "You write books for kids, I figured you would've had some."

"I wanted children." With an effort I unclenched my fingers from around the stem of my wine glass. "But it turns out that I can't have them."

"You can't?" Brooke frowned over that. "Who says?"

I controlled my tone of voice, making sure I sounded matter of fact. "The doctors did."

"Maybe they're wrong." She shrugged it off. "You could always adopt a baby or something by yourself."

Her matter of fact words made me smile. "Maybe I will some day."

Brooke nodded in agreement. "A girl in my class at school is adopted. She said her parents got her from Korea..."

"Brooke—" Garrett tried to intervene.

"I'm going to take Tabby to the litter box," Brooke announced, blissfully unaware of the bomb she'd dropped into the dinner conversation. "Mrs. Huntley said I should make sure Tabby knows where it is." With a clatter of the metal chair across the pavers, she jumped up and went to take the kitten inside.

For a few moments an awkward silence hung over the patio.

"I'm sorry," Garrett began. "She's only a child. She doesn't understand."

"No, that's alright." I studied my plate for a few moments before I lifted my eyes to Garrett's. "I'm overly sensitive to the topic, and that's on me. Not her."

"I'll be honest," Garrett began, "I accidentally overheard most of the circumstances surrounding your divorce last year." His voice was flat, the thoughtful expression on his face had me considering him carefully.

"Oh, and how did you manage that?"

"I was having a meeting with Gabriella at the farmhouse. I think your grandmother was on the phone with you. She was very upset." Smoothly, he topped off the wine in my glass. "Truth be told, your grandmother was pretty damn terrifying."

Despite myself, I began to smile. "I'll bet she

was."

"It was the oddest thing," Garrett said. "But I could have sworn the lights were flickering while she was shouting something about putting a pox on someone named Jared."

I snorted out a laugh, and was perilously close to adoring him.

"I assume Jared would be your ex?"

"That's correct." I picked up my wine.

"Well..." He tapped his glass to mine. "Here's hoping she nailed him."

CHAPTER TEN

There were two flats of lovely pink snapdragons sitting inside my potting shed early the next morning. I did a double take when I opened the shed door and found them waiting for me. A bright yellow delivery slip was sticking out from under one of the flats.

It read: *Garrett picked these out and asked me to deliver. Enjoy, Max.*

I couldn't help it, I stood there with a silly grin on my face and sighed over the snapdragons.

I heard a noise and glanced over my shoulder to find Camilla. Her bubblegum pink hair was tousled artfully. She leaned against the door, and despite the gothic makeup she looked gorgeous. Jeans, a black cropped top and boots completed her rock and roll style outfit. "Did you miss me?" she asked.

"Hey!" I went for a hug. "Are you all set to graduate this weekend?"

"I am." She gave me a squeeze. "Are you ready to have me move back home?"

"Of course," I said. "The house is way too quiet without you living here."

"The gardens look great Dru. I can't believe you accomplished all of this since you moved back."

"I'm about to plant these out front." I hefted a flat of snapdragons. "Would you like to help?"

Cammy snagged a couple of garden trowels, while I loaded the flats into the wheel barrow. She pointed to the gazebo. "Wow, that's different. What magick did you do to it...a cleansing spell maybe?"

"Not quite. I hosed it down with a power washer." I said, making Cammy laugh. "I thought after your graduation ceremony we could have a celebratory barbeque out here."

"Really?" Her face lit up. "I like the sound of that." She followed me around to the front yard.

Sitting in the grass, we started tucking the snaps in the bed all around the pansies and the tulips. I listened with half an ear to my sister talk about her finals. I tried to focus, but I found myself slightly distracted thinking about Garrett, and the amazingly hot kiss he'd given me after he walked me out to my car last night.

I was mortally afraid that I was mooning over him like some teenager. However, we actually had a real date scheduled for the coming evening—just the two of us. Mrs. Huntley had agreed to stay with Brooke, and Garrett and I would be going out to dinner.

It was strange how everything had altered in such a short time. As Ella had said, Garrett had come unexpectedly into my life, and I was indeed falling for him. I was honest enough to admit it.

Part of me wondered how he'd managed to twine his way into my heart so quickly...We'd never even been truly alone for more than a few moments at a time...not yet anyway. *Still,* I thought. *To be seeing a man who was thoughtful, passionate, and romantic. It was all a sort of wonderful magick.*

"I didn't know Max delivered." Cammy's voice broke through my reflections.

"What?" I tuned back in.

Cammy rolled her dramatically outlined eyes. "I said, I didn't know that Max delivered."

I silently continued to plant the flowers.

"Drusilla." Cammy stopped me by pressing a hand on top of mine.

"Yes?" I brushed at my bangs.

"Do you want to tell me about you and Garrett Rivers?"

"Ella," I growled, narrowing my eyes. "Word certainly travels fast."

Camilla let loose a gurgling laugh. "It wasn't Ella. It was Gran. She seems to think she basically engineered the two of you meeting."

I pulled a snapdragon free from a cell pack. "She'd be mistaken."

"So, how serious are things?" Cammy planted a few more flowers.

"We're simply getting to know each other," I said.

"The flowers *are* from him." Cammy nodded at her own deductions.

"He knew I wanted to add some to the gardens, and he asked Max to send them over," I explained. "It was a very thoughtful gesture."

"Romantic too." Cammy raised a single eyebrow. "In the language of flowers snapdragons mean: *you are dazzling, but dangerous.*"

"Yes, I know," I said, and continued to plant the flowers.

"So, is he dazzling, dangerous, or maybe both?"

When I said nothing, Cammy snapped a stalk of the pink flowers and tucked it behind my ear. "I'd keep this close to your skin if I were you."

"Why's that?"

"Having a snapdragon on your person will keep anyone from deceiving you."

I huffed out a breath. "I don't believe that will be necessary at this time, however, the insight certainly might come in handy the next time I deal with my publisher."

"How's the next book coming?" she asked casually.

"I haven't started it yet." I shrugged.

"Good for you." Cammy planted a trio of

snaps. "You need to take some time off, and recoup your personal energy. Reclaim your power."

I eyeballed her. "Have you been speaking to Ella?"

"No. Why?"

"She said something very similar not too long ago."

"We love you Dru," Cammy said quietly but firmly. "All of us want you to be happy."

"I know that." I reached over and gave her hand a squeeze. "Thank you."

***

I changed my dress four times.

Flustered, and sliding towards exasperated, I zipped up the fourth dress. "Damn it." I scowled at my reflection. "I'm not sure about this one either." The simple jersey dress was navy blue. It boasted a floral print, cap sleeves, princess seams, and fell to right below the knee. It was casual, and pretty, but not exactly seduction worthy. *God!* I thought. *I shouldn't even be thinking along those lines.*

Right about the time I was thinking of changing my dress again—Ella poked her head in the room. "That's cute," she said.

"Do you think this navy dress is alright?"

Ella took in the other discarded dresses that were tossed on the bed. "Yes, it's a good choice. Pretty, romantic, and casual."

I blew out a long breath. "Thank you. I couldn't make up my mind."

Ella stuck her head in my closet and pulled out a thin navy cardigan. "Take this along, it will probably be chilly tonight after dinner."

I took the sweater and draped it over my purse. "Good idea." I reached for the discarded dresses and began slipping them back on hangers.

"I'll do that." Ella smoothly took them from me. "Go finish your face."

"It is finished."

Ella frowned. "I think you forgot to put on some blush."

I went to my dresser, squared off with the mirror, and saw that she was right. "Oh for gods sake!" Reaching for the makeup bag, I picked up the blush and dropped it back in the bag.

"I'm nervous," I laughed and leaned against the dresser for support. "Which is ridiculous. I'm twenty-nine years old, and was married for three years. It's not like I've never been on a date before."

My sister walked over to me. "You and Jared never really dated. He swooped in and whisked you off. Before we knew it, you two had eloped and he talked you into moving to Chicago."

I made a face at myself in the mirror. "To be honest, he didn't whisk me away. Yes, I thought I loved him. But I jumped at the chance to get out of Ames Crossing. I was hungry to make something of myself, to launch my career, and I thought Jared with all his connections in publishing would be the person to help me achieve those dreams."

Ella took my hairbrush from the dresser and began to brush my hair down my back. "I think you're being too hard on yourself."

"Maybe," I said, and picked back up the blush. "I'm not sure what this is between Garrett and me, but I think it's for the best to let things progress very slowly."

Ella peeped over my shoulder and met my

eyes in the mirror. "Because you didn't before. I see. That's certainly sensible."

"Yes, it is."

"I wonder, Dru." Ella continued to brush my hair. "Do you suppose the world would end if you decided to simply let things grow and bloom in their own time?"

"Meaning?"

"Stop trying to control everything." Ella gave me a hug. "Some flowers bloom unexpectedly early, or *faster* than others. It doesn't make their contribution to the garden any less important."

I chuckled. "You're using gardening analogies. I'm so proud."

"And I'm proud of you." Ella took my shoulders and turned me to face her. "You are a strong, creative and wise woman. Trust yourself and your instincts a little more."

I leaned my forehead against hers. "I love you, Sis."

Ella gave me a squeeze and then let me go. "And I love you." She pulled a few foil-wrapped packages out of her pocket and slipped them inside my purse.

"Ella, those won't be necessary."

"You never know." Ella winked at me. "Now go out and have an enchanted evening."

The restaurant Garrett chose was a surprise. The formal dining room of the lodge at a nearby state park boasted a gorgeous rustic atmosphere with local stone work and dark wooden beams. There were huge wrap-around windows that allowed for a panoramic view of the river, and a massive limestone fireplace was lit and roaring. With a glimmer of candlelight, the soft voices of the other patrons, and the overall atmosphere, it was casually elegant and intimate.

We talked easily over our meal about the gardens—his and mine, the opening of the winery and the masquerade party they were throwing for the grand opening. I relaxed in his company, even as I admired how wonderful he looked in a gray jacket, a dress shirt open at the throat and his dark slacks. He was a charming dinner companion and he put me at ease, which was the last thing I expected after being nervous to be out with him alone.

As we finished our meal, I toyed with the bud vase that rested on our table and the two purple irises that were arranged inside. "How synchronistic," I said, nodding towards the flowers.

Garrett tipped his head towards them. "Because of the logo for the winery?"

"In the Victorian language of flowers the purple iris says: My compliments," I explained.

"Really?" Garrett slid his hand over mine where it rested on the table. "What else does it say?"

I almost jumped at the contact but managed to control my reaction. It was the first physical contact he'd initiated, other than placing his hand at my back as we'd stepped into the restaurant. *Wait... what had I been talking about?* I tried to remember. *The meanings of the iris.* I yanked my thoughts back in line. "The other meanings of the iris?" I asked him.

His eyes flickered in the candlelight, shifting from blue to aqua. "Yes," he said. "I want to know."

"Classically this flower was a symbol for the Greek Messenger goddess, named Iris." I watched him carefully, wondering how he'd react to the topic. His expression remained open, so I continued. "Iris came down from Olympus on her rainbow to deliver messages from the gods."

He nodded. "And since these flowers come in a rainbow of colors, they named them after the goddess?"

"Exactly." I nodded. "In the wise woman tradition, the flower is associated with communication—as one would expect since it's named after a messenger deity...but the purple iris has other hidden definitions as well."

He skimmed his thumb along my wrist. "Such as?"

With my free hand I lifted my water glass. That caress to my wrist had made my mouth go bone dry. I sipped before I spoke. "The other implications of the flower are ardor, flame, and passion."

"Drusilla," he whispered.

"Yes?" I deliberately set the water glass down, before meeting his eyes.

Their color had deepened, sliding to a dark stormy blue. All the other sounds in the background faded away and once again I found myself entranced by his gaze. My heart began to speed up, and it was as if we were the only two people in the dining room.

Time spun out. I'm not certain how long we sat there lost in each other's eyes, but the spell was suddenly broken by the waiter returning with the check.

Things went back to a more casual tone after dinner, and I wasn't sure if I was relieved or disappointed. As the sun set, Garrett drove me to the Marquette property up on Notch Cliff and gave me a tour of the new winery show room that was very near to opening.

The stone building was charming and put me in mind of a gothic cottage. Inside there was more local stone on the walls, dark stained wainscoting and hardwood floors. There were still boxes and cases of wine to put away, but the checkout and tasting counters were installed. Large wooden wine racks were arranged around the room, Garrett explained, to encourage customers to purchase a bottle or two and take them home.

I spotted wine related gift items displayed on one wall and glasses with the *Trois Amis* logo and name etched on them. After the tour Garrett re-set the alarms, locked up, and we walked under a waxing moon to take in the view.

In the background the Marquette mansion brooded. The fact that scaffolding was two-thirds of the way across the front of the building and renovations were underway didn't stop it from being foreboding or creepy in the least.

"We'll have the masquerade party on the old stone terraces of the house," Garrett explained as we walked along. He pointed out the locations where they planned to put in formal gardens eventually, and a large grassy area where they would erect huge event tents for the night of the party.

"Gran and Ella have been talking about the party, they're very excited about the grand opening," I said, pulling my cardigan closer to ward off the wind.

"And you?" Garrett gave my hand a gentle squeeze. "Are you looking forward to it, Drusilla?"

I tilted my head up and studied the gothic stone house. It had been three stories tall at one point. But an entire wing had caved in. "That house still gives me the heebie-jeebies. All we'd need is the crashing waves on the rocky shores of Maine and it'd be a dead ringer for Collinwood Manor."

Garrett chuckled and slipped an arm around my shoulders. "You mean from the old *Dark Shadows* show?"

"Yes, exactly." I nodded. "According to Cammy, there's already a ghost in residence." The wind moaned through the old trees, and I checked nervously over my shoulder. "Maybe you could put that in your brochures. It would probably bump up the number of tourists to your winery...simply from the paranormal interest factor alone."

"It is a little creepy I suppose," Garrett said, "but it never bothered Philippe. He's been living here during the restoration."

"You mean he sleeps inside that house?" I shuddered, studying the one remaining stone tower. "I hope he keeps ropes of garlic nearby."

Garrett frowned at first, then he began to chuckle. "Oh, garlic. To ward off the vampires."

"You have to admit, that decrepit old house

looks like it *would* have a vampire lurking around."

Garrett grinned and tucked me under his arm. "I can't wait to introduce you to Philippe. You'll be just his type."

"You better not mean blood type," I said dryly.

I smiled as Garrett tossed back his head and laughed.

"It is beautiful here," Garrett's voice was quiet now as we surveyed the river far below. "I felt this connection the first time the three of us walked the property." He sighed. "I would have never imagined back then that I'd be raising Brooke—and Barry and Melissa would be gone."

"I'm sorry about Barry and your cousin," I said quietly. "I wish I would have had the chance to have known them."

"Melissa was great." Garrett's voice was filled with emotion. "She was fun, sassy, and kept Barry from being too serious."

In sympathy I laid my head on his shoulder and tucked my arm around his waist. We silently gazed out over the cliffs with the ruins of the house to our backs.

A waxing crescent moon hovered to the west. We stood there watching it set, and listened to the night sounds. When Garrett lowered his mouth to mine it was exactly right, and I felt for the first time in several years, a belonging of sorts.

By the time Garrett drove me home it was late. He'd been somewhat quiet since we'd left Notch Cliff, but as he walked me towards the porch, he'd reached for me, and I went willingly into his arms for a kiss goodnight.

Eventually, he pulled away. "I'm trying to give you that time you asked for."

I was intending to say goodnight when I saw a flash out of the corner of my eyes. "Lightning bugs," I breathed. A pair of fireflies were dancing in and out of the hedges and were headed towards the back gardens. It was about a month sooner than I'd expected to see them, but the fact that I did thrilled me.

"Garrett." I reached for him. "Come and see." Taking his hand, I led him into the back gardens. My Gran's prized hydrangeas were starting to bloom and there were a dozen lightning bugs flashing in and out of the blooming shrubs.

"It's gorgeous back here, almost like a faerie-tale," Garrett said. "It's hard to believe what you've accomplished this spring."

"It was a lot of work, but the gardens are coming back," I said quietly. "The hydrangeas are blooming early this year." I thought about what Ella had said, about flowers blooming unexpectedly and my heart slammed hard against my ribs once, and then it settled. *It was time,* I realized. *Time to take a step forward and to reclaim my power. With this man, tonight.*

Set in the farthest section of the gardens, the gazebo was wreathed in shadows and would allow for some privacy. I peeked up at him and led him across the yard with the solar lights softly illuminating the way for us. I took a seat on one of the wooden benches built around the interior perimeter of the gazebo, sat my purse to the side, and patted the spot next to me.

"I was wondering," I began as he sat. "We're having a barbeque for Cammy's graduation this Sunday. Would you and Brooke like to attend?"

"Are you asking me on a date?" One side of

his mouth kicked up.

"Yes." I smiled. "I suppose I am."

"Yes," he said. "I'm sure Brooke and I would both enjoy that."

"I had a wonderful time tonight," I said, and took his hand.

"So did I." He turned my hand over and pressed a gentle kiss to the back of it. "I should go."

"The night's not over yet," I said, and watched as his eyes flashed electric blue in the darkness. "Don't go, Garrett."

"Drusilla." He dropped his forehead against mine.

"Kiss me," I whispered, lifting my mouth to his.

Gently, he pulled me closer. As we kissed, the stars twinkled in the midnight sky and the lightning bugs flickered around us. I felt his left hand skim over my back, and down lower to the outside of my calf. He slowly trailed his fingers up to my knee, and then he hesitated when he reached the hem of my dress.

"Drusilla, I want you." His voice rasped in my ear. "I have since the first moment I saw you standing in the rain at the river's edge."

I pulled back a bit to meet his eyes. "The first time I saw you, I thought you were a water spirit, or a Selkie who'd taken human form." I said. "But I have a writer's imagination."

I could see his smile flash even in the darkness. "Kiss me," he whispered.

I lifted my mouth to his, and when he kissed me again, I opened my lips to his fully. His kiss was hot, demanding, and thrilled me down to my toes. When his fingers gripped my knee, I moaned and moved against him.

He stopped again, pulling back to look me in the eyes. "Is that a yes?" he demanded, his voice low and rough.

"Absolutely, yes," I breathed.

Garrett picked me right up from the bench and carried me to the hidden, grassy area behind the gazebo. Setting me on my feet, he shrugged his jacket off and spread it out on the ground. Garrett swooped in for a hard kiss, and slowly we eased our way down to the spring grass. I felt a thrill as he laid me back against the jacket. While our kiss went on and on, I felt the cool night air brush against my thighs as he pushed the fabric of my skirt up and out of his way.

Garrett traced a lazy pattern of kisses down my chest, across my hip, and finally along the outside of my thigh. One of his hands was busy teasing and tormenting my breasts, while the other had slipped under the edge of my panties. I shuddered, allowing my legs to fall open for him.

I almost jolted straight off the ground when he slipped his fingers past my practical cotton underwear and touched me.

"Easy now," he crooned, and I had only begun to breathe again when he turned his head and sweetly kissed the inside of my knee.

"Oh god," I managed. *I should be practical and tell him I had protection in my purse,* I thought. *I should...*

My thoughts trailed off as he trailed kisses down the inside of my thigh, and I was completely caught off guard when he pulled my panties aside with one hard yank; and dipped his head to taste me..

My back arched off the ground in pleasure. I sank my fingers in his hair and held him to me.

I was lost in sensations. My heart felt like it was going to burst through my chest and he growled a little against me, and the vibration almost tipped me over the edge. "Garrett," I panted, half sitting up. "Garrett." I tugged his hair to get his attention. "It's been a long time for me. If you do that again I won't last."

He stopped. I could see his eyes in the darkness, and what I saw there had me trembling. "Shh," he ran one hand along the side of my face. "Lie back for me," he ordered.

I pressed a kiss to the palm of his hand and acquiesced. He tugged my panties down and off, and I watched as he slowly unbuttoned his shirt. I whispered to him that I had protection in my purse, and he left me only long enough to go and fetch it. When he returned, I reached for him.

"No," he said with a little smile. "Don't distract me."

"But I want to touch you," I whispered.

A slow smile spread over his face as he unbuckled and unzipped in front of me. I started to reach for him; but he ran his hands up my thighs, wrapped his hands around my bottom, and lifted my hips.

I caught my breath as he gradually lowered his head. I started to shake in reaction as his tongue tormented and teased—lightly and slowly at first. Then he claimed me with open mouth kisses and firm strokes of his tongue. I felt his fingers push gently inside and when he growled against me again, I went straight over the edge, seeing stars as the orgasm went on and on. It took everything I had not to scream my pleasure to the skies.

Slowly he allowed my hips to return to the ground. I fought to catch my breath as Garrett eased between my legs. He nudged my thighs farther apart and before I could blink the stars from my eyes; he pressed smoothly forward, sliding deep inside.

Garrett held me motionless in a tight grip for a few moments as my feminine muscles adjusted to his invasion. It was exquisite, it was almost too much, and I wanted more. He cupped my face in one of his hands as I lay there trembling. "Are you alright?" His voice was ragged, and I could tell he was holding himself in check.

While I appreciated his restraint and care, it had been far, far too long for me. I reached out for him and dug my fingernails in his hips. "Garrett!" I urged him on.

"More?" he gritted out, holding perfectly still.

I started to tremble all over. "God, yes!"

"Hold on." Was all the warning I got. He looped his arms under my knees and slung his hips forward at the same time. He began to move harder and faster, and with an intensity that left me breathless. I held on and enjoyed the wild ride.

Afterwards, we lay together. Spooned up against his side, I blinked sleepily at what I saw. *There were stars dancing all around us,* I thought. Then I figured out I was actually seeing lighting bugs.

"Garrett, look," I whispered, pointing up.

The fireflies flashed through the garden and wove in and out of the hydrangeas. I sighed as they began to fly directly over the two of us. Garrett pulled me a bit closer and we watched the lightning bugs do a lazy waltz in the air.

Here, in the deep shadows of the yard I felt

the magick. The garden, I realized had given us its blessing.

CHAPTER ELEVEN

I was woken up with soft kisses and softer words.

"Drusilla," he said, kissing my eyelids and making me smile.

I sighed happily and snuggled closer.

"It's late. I should go." Garrett slowly sat up and began to straighten his clothes.

I shivered a bit. The nighttime air was chilly, and the grass was now uncomfortably wet from dew.

He took my hand and I rose to my feet, taking his jacket with me. I handed it back to him. It was crumpled, damp, and blades of grass clung to it. "Sorry about your jacket."

He leaned over and kissed me. "I'm not."

I smoothed my wrinkled dress down, and when he held his hand out to me again, I took it. Together, we silently walked around to the front of the house.

We kissed goodnight and lingered at his car. I didn't want him to go, but we had to be practical. "I'll see you and Brooke at the barbeque for Cammy this weekend?"

"Unless I can figure out a way to see you sooner." He kissed me on the forehead, then pulled me close. "I don't want to leave," he said against my hair.

"It's alright," I said. "I understand, you need to get home to Brooke." I opened his car door for him and nudged him inside.

He started the car and rolled down the driver's window. "You distracted me earlier." He leaned out the window. "I had planned to ask you to accompany me to the masquerade party for the grand opening of the winery."

"Yes, of course I will." I smiled when he took my hand and pressed a kiss to the back of it. "I'll look forward to it."

"Goodnight, Drusilla," he said, and began to ease his car out of the driveway.

"Goodnight." I stayed where I was and watched him drive away. I'd never expected to fall in love again... yet here I was, starting to anyway. I felt something fall against my bare feet and discovered the late-blooming pink tulips had bent over.

"A dreamy love," I giggled at the message of the flowers. Hugging my arms across my chest, I practically skipped along the path to the front door.

My sister had guessed right, Garrett Rivers was an intense lover...and I *did* wonder how soon it would be until we could do it all over again.

***

The next week passed quickly, and Garrett and I managed to see each other once or twice, but we were never alone. I dropped by his house one day with a big strawberry pot I'd planted with culinary herbs for Mrs. Huntley's birthday. The housekeeper loved it, and she put it in a sunny spot right outside of the kitchen door.

We went to the movies together with Brooke, and I wondered how she would react over the new dynamic, but Garrett informed me that he'd spoken to her and Brooke's response to us dating was a big grin, and the casual pronouncement that it was "awesome".

As we shuffled down the aisle to take our seats in the theatre he tucked an arm around my waist, and Brooke rolled her eyes asking us not to make out in front of her while we were in public. But she grinned when she said it, and I took that as a good sign.

We kept in touch mostly by phone and text. I knew things were insanely hectic for him at the moment, with it only being a matter of days before the winery opened. Between that and Cammy's pending graduation we were both busy. But I found myself missing him.

I toyed with an idea for my next book, and when Cammy's graduation day rolled around, I sat in the auditorium with Ella and Gran and cheered, watching my youngest sister walk across the stage to receive her Master's degree.

After the ceremony, Gran of course wanted pictures of me and my sisters together. Once that was finished, we loaded up all of Cammy's things from her college apartment into our cars and headed back to Ames Crossing. Cammy moved into the room across the hall from mine, and the house felt full to bursting with all four of us living together in it again.

Sunday dawned with mild temperatures and partly sunny skies. While Ella and Gran prepped the food to feed our guests, Cammy and I decorated the gazebo with streamers and balloons, in my sister's signature colors of pink and black.

I stood on the wooden bench of the gazebo, taping the last of the streamers in place. "This color pink almost matches your hair," I said, dropping the roll of tape into the pocket of my new sundress. I ran a hand down over the skirt. Cheerful sunflowers were splashed across a white background, and I thought it was a good choice for a party in the garden. It was practical, romantic and comfortable with a tank-style top, soft fabric and high waist.

"Something's different out here." Cammy flipped out a long plastic tablecloth in hot pink. "I'm picking up some *very* interesting vibes," she said, smoothing the tablecloth over the long table.

I climbed down from the bench and went to arrange Gran's old wooden folding chairs around the table. "Oh?" I asked.

"Yeah..." Cammy narrowed her eyes, held her hands out in front and began walking around the perimeter of the gazebo.

Tucking a chair in, I eyeballed my witchy sister. She did look the part in her celestial patterned black, skater-style dress. "Cammy, what in the world are you doing?"

"I'm trying to sense where all this energy is coming from."

"You're not going to start chanting, are you?"

"Would you like me too?" she replied. "Come to think of it, that might be helpful while I scan for the energy."

"Is what you're doing a metaphysical type of radar or something?" I asked, amused at my sister's antics.

"Oh ye of little faith," Cammy quipped.

I watched, amazed as she went directly to the spot where Garrett and I had been kissing the other night on the bench. *There's no way she could know...*

"Wow," her breath whistled out. "That's some smoking hot residual energy!" She kept her hands out in front of her, and unerringly retraced our steps to where Garrett and I had lain in the grassy area behind the gazebo. "And there's even more over here...Wowsers!" she announced.

"We should see if Gran and Ella need any help with the food," I said, trying to distract her.

"And what's this?" She turned and walked over to the nearby hydrangea bushes. "You know, the hydrangea symbolizes *remembrance*. But I'd say someone didn't get the message... and accidentally left something behind."

"What?" Despite myself, I followed her. To my absolute mortification, Cammy bent down, reached under the hydrangeas, and pulled out a pair of white cotton panties. I gasped, and felt the blood rush to my cheeks.

Cammy raised her eyes to my face, shifted her attention to the underwear dangling from her fingers, and then slowly slid her gaze back to me. "Drusilla Anne Midnight!" She sounded scandalized.

I folded my arms across my chest

defensively. "They're not mine," I lied.

Cammy waved the underwear. "You shameless hussy!"

I rolled my eyes. "Oh for goodness sake."

Cammy burst out laughing, chucked the underwear, and grabbed me up into a big hug. "I've never been more proud in my entire life!"

"Shut up, Cammy."

She pulled back and held me at arm's length. "So how was he?" she wanted to know.

"How was who?" I played dumb.

"Don't mess with me, Drusilla." Cammy lifted her right eyebrow. "It had to have been Garrett Rivers."

"Please." I stared down my nose. "I'm not the type of woman who brags about her sexual escapades."

"You said 'sexual escapades'." Cammy's lips twitched. "So...was it escapade-ish?"

I did my best not to laugh. It would only encourage her. "We need to get ready. Your company will be here in an hour."

"Nope." She tightened her grip. "Spill the details first."

"I absolutely will not."

"You can trust me. I'm the soul of discretion," she swore, her green eyes twinkling. "Tell me two things. Just two things."

"If I must."

"You must," she insisted.

"Fine." I said. "One: In the garden. Two: Under the stars."

"How was it?" she demanded, searching my face.

"Honestly? It was amazing," I said.

"Seriously, I'm dying to know...was he all tender and sweet, silent and intense, or did he spank your ass and pull your hair?"

I bit my lip. "There was *no* ass spanking," I said as soberly as possible.

"Of course, of course." Cammy let go of my arms and fluffed her pink hair. "A girl's got to save something for the honeymoon."

That did it. I couldn't hold it back anymore and a helpless laugh snorted out. That only made my sister giggle, and we both ended up leaning against each other and laughing like lunatics.

Cammy stayed true to her word, and when

everyone arrived for the barbeque she greeted Garrett and Brooke cordially. Garrett wore his khaki slacks and a sporty blue polo shirt very well. Brooke was wearing shorts, a purple shirt, and her hair was braided down her back.

I was surprised when Garrett came directly to me and kissed me on the mouth. He didn't linger over it too long. But the message was clear—he let everyone know without a word that we were a couple. My eyes flashed nervously to Brooke, but she simply grinned at me and flashed a thumbs up.

I looked around at Ella talking with Max, Cammy chatting with her friends, and Gran holding court in a padded lawn chair. She motioned Garrett and I over to her.

"Uh-oh," I said. "We've been summoned."

Garrett took my hand and kissed it. The romantic, old fashioned gesture thrilled me straight to my toes.

Gran sat in her Adirondack chair, wearing Bermuda shorts, a bright plaid blouse and sassy cat eye sunglasses. She sipped her drink from a long straw and waved us over to take a seat next to her. "Sit down," she ordered. "I'm not craning my neck to talk to you."

Garrett and I took the wooden bench that I'd painted a deep midnight blue a few weeks before. "Gran..." I began.

She held up a hand, and I fell to silence. "Drusilla, Garrett. I simply wanted to say that it's lovely to see you two together."

"Thank you," Garrett said formally.

Gran's eyes slid over to where Brooke stood talking with Ella and Max. "Brooke seems much happier."

"She is," Garrett agreed.

"Good." Gran nodded. "That girl has been one of ours from the first moment she stepped foot in the Midnight family gardens a year ago. I'm relieved to see her doing so well."

"As am I," Garrett said.

Gran smiled. "Now, why don't you two go enjoy yourselves. Have some food and a drink."

We stood, recognizing the royal dismissal, as it were. "Can I get you anything, Gran?" I asked.

"I'd love a beer," she said. "I'm not some invalid to sit in the shade and sip at lemonade all day."

"I'll take care of that for you," Garrett said, and went to the coolers.

My Gran gave my hand a squeeze as I left. I wandered over toward the faery gardens, and Brooke raced over to join me.

"Hey Dru!" she waved her pink cast. "The doctor says this gets to come off next week."

"That's wonderful!"

Brooke bent over and plucked a pansy. She laid it over the statue's book, as an offering. "How is Bluebell doing? Have you written her a new story yet?"

"You sound like my editor." I rolled my eyes. "She's been hounding me for the past few weeks."

"Maybe I can help you with the new story." Brooke glanced up shyly.

"Actually, I think you already have."

"Oh yeah? How?"

"I'm planning to introduce a new character into my series," I said. "I've been tossing the idea around for the past week or so."

"Tell me," Brooke demanded.

"I was thinking about adding a red-haired faerie who is cranky, lonely, and a little lost.

But Bluebell and the other faeries in the garden would help her heal and become happy again."

Brooke laughed. "Maybe you could name her after me."

I gave her a one-armed hug. "I think I'll have to."

"Brooke?" Gran called.

"Yes, Ma'am?" Brooke swung her head around.

Gran motioned her over. "Come sit by me and tell me all about that new kitten of yours."

Brooke skipped over and sat next to my grandmother.

Garrett returned to my side and slipped an arm around my waist. "I've said it before, the gardens are stunning. You've done an amazing job bringing them back to life."

We strolled over to the formal herb garden. "I think they've helped me almost as much as I did them."

Garrett gave my waist a warm squeeze. "Would you be offended if I told you I preferred them at night?"

I grinned even as the foliage from the feverfew plants brushed across my bare toes. "I agree, there is a certain magick that only can be experienced at midnight, under the stars."

"Drusilla." He dropped a kiss on my mouth, his aqua-blue eyes shifted colors as he searched my face. "I think it's only fair to let you know...I'm falling in love with you."

My heart trembled in my chest, and for a moment I couldn't speak. I nodded and hunkered down to pluck a few blossoms from the formal herb bed. I took a steadying breath while I was kneeling by the herbs and tried to compose myself.

"Drusilla." Gently he took my hand and helped me rise. "Did you hear what I said?"

I sniffed the tiny daisy like flowers. "I did."

"What do have to say to that?"

I twirled the stem in my hand. "In the language of flowers, the feverfew has a very specific message," I explained, taking the feverfew blossoms and tucking them in the buttonhole of his shirt.

"Oh?" Garrett glanced down at the flowering herb and back to me.

"It means: Love, I return your affection." I gave his hand a squeeze.

Garrett began to smile, then he drew me in his arms, dipped me back, and kissed me in front of everyone. As we kissed in the bright May sunshine, surrounded by the gardens and our friends and family, I felt happy and at peace.

However, this isn't the end of our story, it's only the beginning...

Keep reading for a preview of Daughters Of Midnight, Book 2,

Midnight Masquerade

Midnight Masquerade
Daughters Of Midnight, Book Two

I'd made up my mind.

I was going to tell Max Dubois how I felt about him. I'd waited for the perfect occasion, and a romantic opportunity had at last presented itself. I, Gabriella Midnight, mild mannered graphic designer, the quiet and dependable middle sister of the daughters of Midnight, was *finally* going to go and get her man.

The party for the *Trois Amis* Winery's grand opening was only a few days away, and I was frantically trying to find something amazing to wear. After all, if I was going to sweep a man off his feet, I needed to set the stage for seduction...so to speak.

Now, I was scouting the shops with my younger sister, hoping that I might stumble across a dress I could turn into something worthy of a fancy masquerade party. I'd procrastinated, as usual, and had put off going dress shopping until the last minute. As I worked my way through the evening gowns on a sales rack, I felt a touch of panic over the lack of worthy options.

Nope. No. Dear god no... With a cringe I thought about all of the gorgeous romance novel covers I'd designed in the past few years and wondered why *I* wasn't finding an evening gown that captured my imagination. I needed an amazing sale price and a bit of magick, if I hoped to pull off wooing the man of my dreams. I frowned over a sequined red slip dress, dismissed it as too Jessica Rabbit, and wondered if it was possible to find anything worthy of an enchanted evening.

"Ella!" my sister Cammy called to me.

I swung my head around and discovered she was waving me over. I put the red number back on the rack.

"I found some prom dresses on sale!" Cammy said excitedly.

I balked. "Prom dresses?" I frowned at her.

"I'm twenty-seven years old. I'm not wearing a prom dress."

"Prom dress, bridesmaid dress, evening gown, what does it matter? Between the two of us, we can find something and make it work," Cammy said from over the mound of taffeta and tulle that was bundled in her arms. She shoved me towards a dressing room. "Let's try these on."

I was stuffed in a dressing room before I could blink. My sister, shy retiring thing that she was, came right in with me. I sighed. "Jeez, Cammy."

"What?" She raised a single brow. "I think I may have found something I can use too."

Rolling my eyes to the ceiling, I peeled off my clothes and began trying on dresses. The first one was hot pink in shimmery taffeta. The dress was too slim fitting and it put way too much emphasis on my hips and butt. Both of which I hated. "Oh, hell no," I muttered, scowling at my reflection.

Cammy peered over my shoulder, her bubblegum pink hair clashed wildly with the color of the one-shoulder dress I had on. "I agree. The color is bad and the fit isn't flattering. That's a no." She spun and presented her back. "Zip me up, will ya?"

I tugged the zipper on her black dress that had a simple off the shoulder top and a massive explosion of a skirt. The netting was a very fine texture, and the length of the A-line skirt fell to right above her ankles.

"I think that's a little too short for you," I said.

"No, it's not short enough." Cammy considered her reflection in the mirror. "I'm thinking I might cut it off to right above my knees, maybe add some star appliques, and a few sequins on the netting of the skirt."

I nodded. "That's a great idea."

"It's a bargain for forty bucks." Cammy grinned. "Come on Ella, try on something else."

"Why am I not surprised that you went for the witchy, black dress?"

"It contrasts nicely with my hair."

I reached for the next gown. It was a pale dusty blue. "I like the style of this one."

"I thought it might look good with your coloring."

While Cammy changed back into her clothes I struggled with the blue dress. I managed to get my arms in the sleeves, and then got stuck trying to ease it over my head. "A little help please!" My voice was muffled under layers of tulle.

"Hang on." Cammy came around and started tugging the dress down.

It slipped into place. I checked the mirror and was pleasantly surprised. The gown was romantic, with long sheer sleeves. The off-the-shoulder style was actually flattering. The bodice was a tad snug, but it made my waist look smaller. The tulle skirt poofed out, effectively hiding my butt, and the long skirt swept down to the floor with a bit of a flounce at the hem.

"I dig this one!" Cammy said, looking at my reflection in the mirror. "Your waist looks tiny, and it has a definite Cinderella vibe."

This could work... I considered the dress, but I noticed a tear in the flounce. "It's torn, though."

Cammy knelt down. "It's on the seam. I can fix this easily."

I checked the tag hanging from the sleeve. It was seventy percent off. "I like the price."

Cammy stood behind me and scooped up my long blonde hair. "You should wear your hair up, with a little bit of your curls falling in tendrils."

This dress definitely sets an old fashioned, dreamy, and sort of faery tale tone... I smiled at my reflection in the mirror. "I don't even look like myself in this."

My little sister grinned at me. "Isn't that the whole point of the masquerade party?"

I turned back to the mirror. *Max was never going to know what hit him,* I decided.

Midnight Masquerade
Coming June 2018

ABOUT THE AUTHOR

Ellen Dugan is the award winning author of over twenty five books. Ellen's popular non-fiction titles have been translated into over twelve foreign languages. She branched out successfully into paranormal fiction in 2015 with her popular "Legacy Of Magick" series, and has been featured in USA TODAY'S HEA column. Ellen lives an enchanted life in Missouri. Please visit her website and blog:

www.ellendugan.com
www.ellendugan.blogspot.com

77756299R00128

Made in the USA
Middletown, DE
25 June 2018